SINNER'S SAINT

LEIGHANN HART

PLAYLIST

Sorry - Our Last Night
Tell Me You Love Me - Andie Case
Back in Your Head - Tegan and Sara
Take Me to Church - Hozier
Call Me - Shinedown
The Chain - Fleetwood Mac
The Kind and All of His Men - Wolf Gang
Love the Way You Lie - Eminem, Rihanna
Somebody That I Used to Know - Gotye, Kimbra
Hello - Adele
Torn - Hands Like Houses
Can't Feel My Face - The Weeknd
Saying Sorry - Hawthorne Heights
Motion Sickness - Phoebe Bridgers
Cardiac Arrest - Bad Suns
Breezeblocks - alt-J
Like a Fool - Kiera Knightley
California Dreamin' - The Mamas & The Papas
Soul Meets Body - Death Cab for Cutie
Devour - Marilyn Manson
Possum Kingdom - Toadies
Better Now - Post Malone
The Pretender - Foo Fighters
Stand By Me - Florence + The Machine
Avalanche - Leonard Cohen
Clarity - Zedd, Foxes
Paranoia in B Major - The Avett Brothers
Cold Cold Cold - Cage the Elephant
All We Ever Knew - The Head and The Heart

Something to Believe In - Young the Giant
Young Bride - Midlake
Gods & Monsters - Lana Del Rey
Last to Know - Three Days Grace
You Make Me Wanna Die - The Shivas
Toes - Glass Animals
In Cold Blood - alt-J
At Last - Etta James
Hate Me - Ellie Goulding, Juice WRLD
October - Broken Bells, Danger Mouse
When You Can't Sleep at Night - Of Mice & Men
Light My Love - Greta Van Fleet

"And we all know love is a glass which makes even a monster appear fascinating."

— **ALBERTO MORAVIA,** *THE WOMAN OF ROME*

August

1
K.O.

Dayton

*D*ayton,
    Seeing as you're the furthest thing from a professional, I will no longer refer to you using your prestigious title.

You're a sick, twisted fuck.

I'm appalled that your resignation was at your own hand and not Dean Raza's doing. You're a cowardly bastard if you thought resigning and setting up shop in the next town over would erase me, would erase your problems. You must have lost your hideously diseased mind, "darling."

And to think, I almost fell for you, believing I knew what you were capable of, only to find out I didn't know you at all. Not for a second. You made love to me and you were so raw, so real, you managed to convince me that your feelings were genuine.

What a brilliant actor you were.

I'm penning this letter to make something clear: I know everything. I found your disgusting little box.

I shouldn't have been so surprised by it—the other girls tried to warn

1

me. Even in the early days, I suppose your ineffable charm swayed me. I ignored their warnings. I allowed myself to get closer and closer to you until I was blinded to how dangerous you truly are. Until I lifted that lid, anyway.

As much as those photographs turned my stomach, your dedication to making me stand out among the rest was far more off-putting. So I left. Now you know. Although, you've probably figured that out already, you brilliant bastard.

Do you blame me? What was I to do, stick around and be your patron saint of sluts?

And despite all of this rage, all of the hate etched into the lines of this letter, and even though you wrecked my summer and ripped away my chance of participating in my own graduation ceremony, I don't want revenge.

What I want is quite simple: this job.

If you fail to supply me with the position, I should forewarn you that revenge becomes the unfortunate plan B.

You see, even in my state of shock that fateful morning in your bedroom, I mustered enough calm to capture my own photographic evidence of your perverted trophy box.

The entire summer, an email to the Oregon Medical Board has been sitting in my draft folder. With attachments. Give me your decision before the week is out or I may accidentally hit send.

I'll be seeing you. Soon, I hope, for your sake.

-K.O.

How appropriate of Kenna to sign her initials on such a letter. K.O., indeed. The poor girl probably thought she had signed his death warrant. She hadn't. Far from it.

If his career was suddenly wrecked by her little email, nothing was tying him to Oregon. He'd move out of state, change his identity, gain employment in a city that was small and quaint where they wouldn't ask questions about the reserved doctor from the West Coast.

Except, that was all a lie.

She was tying him here, the woman Dayton had spent the entire summer trying to forget. Kenna had stopped his eight-year-long research project in its tracks and with her he'd fallen accidentally and hopelessly in love.

Gingerly, he set the letter on his desk.

It posed no threat to him, he decided. The only harm here lay in her poisonous words. He could handle her ire as long as it meant she would eventually come around.

Delicacy had to be employed. A muted hopefulness sprang to life in his sternum as he mulled over the possibilities. He would offer her the position, as she had proposed, and she'd believe she had the upper hand. All the while oblivious to the fact that he wasn't intimidated by her attempt at blackmail. He imagined her scent and notebooks and lipstick-stained coffee cups littering the practice. She would be back in his office, where she belonged.

Where he'd lure Kenna back into his arms.

Dayton pulled out his cell phone, thumb dancing across the display, and soon the dial tone purred in his ear.

2

YOU WIN, KID

Kenna

*I*mpregnated gray clouds sulked beyond the university bookstore's windows. Despite the tension, the weight, something held back the rain.

Kenna had parted ways with that feeling. She'd been cast the victim all her life, with her family, with Reid, and then Dayton. That part of her was dead. Gone.

She intended to show him that she wasn't some naive, weak girl who was easily manipulated. Summer was fading into fall, an entire season separating them, and the tables had turned. She had seen his 'help wanted' ads around town and it wasn't a matter of if she'd apply, but when, and though the daunting errand of hand-delivering the application to his office mailbox had required several days of recuperation, she teemed with triumph in the end.

A surge of power coursed through her as she stalked along the psychology aisle, fingers lazily swiping across the spines of books as she went, feeling like a femme fatale. She considered her good fortune. Grad school started next week and the man who'd wronged her was helpless in the face of her demands. The sense of power, the certainty and control attached to it, was soothing.

Until it morphed into guilt.

Dayton had caused her suffering, yes, but instead of healing, forgiving, and moving on, her heart insisted on vengeance. She wanted to watch him suffer as she'd been made to. But what would it solve? It was then she knew that corrupt line of thinking was his influence. Kenna sought out confessional every week that summer, fearing he had stained her heart with malevolence—something black and festering and impossible to evict.

What kept her awake at night was not the bitterness that had invaded her soul but rather what was buried beneath it, the fluttering in her stomach when she hovered over Dayton's contact info on her phone or the racing of her pulse every time she saw the dead bouquet of garnet roses that still adorned her dresser. Petals black and crisp with no chance of revival.

On days she stared long enough, whether it was a trick of the light or pure hallucination, she swore new growth emerged on the dry stems; tiny, blossoming leaves clinging to a life that had been predestined to fail.

"Am I looking in the wrong place for Psych 101 or am I just going crazy?" Liza's buttery voice cut through her inner monologue, reminding her that she wasn't alone on the textbook shopping crusade.

Her big, whiskey-colored eyes locked on Kenna from where she stood on the other side of the waist-height bookshelf, long lashes brushing her square brows.

Alex had moved back to Phoenix following the completion of her M.F.A. program. The day she left, they'd shared a crushing hug in the parking lot of their apartment complex where her ride to the airport was waiting. She had urged Kenna to 'stay out of trouble' before shedding a few tears and slipping into the backseat. She watched as Alex rode away in that car, not knowing what she knew.

The box. The perversion.

And though keeping that hideous secret had weighed her down like a ton of steel, it was better that way.

There was nothing left for Alex in Branch Spring. She belonged in Arizona, with her family. She'd settle into her new life, her career, and one day—with any luck—Dayton Merino would be a distant memory.

Liza Singh had proved to be a decent roommate in the three months they'd shared an apartment. She was clean, and quiet. They stayed out of each other's way. Kenna knew their true test of compatibility would come with the start of fall semester, when stress levels spiked and responsibilities were in full swing.

Kenna blew at the little sprigs of hair that had sprung free from her bun before flashing a reassuring smile. "No, you're not crazy. You know who's crazy? The people who stock this place. Go comb the sociology section and report back."

"Sociology? Seriously?"

She mouthed 'I know.' Her basket had filled up a while ago but she was in no hurry to leave. Something delightfully infectious lurked within the bookstore, the prospect of rain and the endless possibilities of a new term on the horizon.

The gentle thrum of her phone vibrating against her thigh rooted Kenna to the spot. Everything unfolded in slow motion as she retrieved it from her pocket. She dared a look at the caller ID and it felt like her breath had been cut off.

A covert glance to the left showed that Liza lingered several aisles away. It was safe to answer.

But did she want to?

Accepting the call would send Lucifer's voice slithering into her ear. All of that control she'd held in such high esteem crumbled as she stared at the white letters spanning her screen. *Dr. Merino.*

Hand shaking, she managed, "Talk."

"You win, kid. Send me your schedule."

Click.

His speech was concise but she felt as though he'd reached through the phone and seized her throat. Struck by the dizzying aftermath of a thousand pirouettes, Kenna grabbed onto the nearest shelf for support and as she gripped its cool metal, everything around her spun, reducing the bookstore to swipes of light and color.

Dayton was operating under the assumption that she'd get his medical license revoked if he didn't give her the job. What he didn't know was that she had already sought out another avenue for justice.

The Branch Spring Police Department.

They'd informed her nothing could be done about the Polaroids—she may not have had the actual copies, but she came armed with documented evidence on her phone—citing that they were a far cry from criminal activity. When Kenna told the officers the photos belonged to a well-respected man in the community, they more or less laughed in her face and shoved her out the precinct's door.

But the malice in Dayton's tone suggested that, to him, the threat against his career, his freedom, was alive and well.

He was no fool. Surely, he knew nothing would happen to him and that thought had Kenna ready to regurgitate her breakfast on the linoleum floor.

If he realized he was out of harm's way, he must have had an angle for hiring her. The idea alone was terrifying.

"Are you feeling alright, Ace?" Liza reappeared in her khaki raincoat, waving a hand in front of Kenna's face. "You don't look so hot."

Ever since uncovering her middle name, Liza had affectionately adopted the nickname 'Ace.' Kenna might have been miffed by this if Liza had any competing annoying qualities, of which there were none. Unless one counted her fascination with reality television.

Shutting her eyes, Kenna held her forehead and siphoned a great breath before they walked in tandem to the checkout line. "Yeah, I—I might lie down for a bit when we get home."

Liza's head snapped in her direction, her thick, black braid swishing at her backside. "Who were you on the phone with, just now?"

"News about a job."

"Good news?"

She had yet to decide if serving as Dayton's underling five days a week qualified as good or bad news.

They moved several spots closer to the registers.

"I got the job so, good, I guess."

Liza had more to say, evident in the probing mask that slipped over her face. The same one she wore while inquiring about the dead flowers on the dresser or why Kenna never called her family. Things she didn't want to discuss.

Eyes glimmering, Liza tilted her body toward her. The decibel level at which she spoke scarcely clocked in at a whisper. "This may not be the best venue to tell you this, but I've been worried about you lately so I'm just going to say it. Over the summer, there were rumors. People are talking about you."

"I know." Her basket felt heavier by the minute. The line, unmoving.

"Is it true? About you and this Dr.—"

"Please, don't say his name. You shouldn't believe everything you hear around campus. It's dead around here. Everyone's looking for gossip, even if it means creating it."

The lines reminded her of what she had said to Professor Henrick the day he'd informed her she would be spending her summer redoing her mentorship.

They had not gained any validity over the months.

It was no longer gossip. Everyone knew.

Liza's lips parted slightly, no doubt ready with another question, and Kenna had never been more grateful than the moment the cashier called 'next.' She rushed forth and surrendered her textbooks.

Free of all weight, real and imagined.

3

BAD SEED

Dayton

*T*alk.

One word, one syllable was all Kenna had graced him with, but to his desperate ears it carried the beauty and precision of a Mozart sonata.

He stared at the phone resting in his palm, her information filling the display. Had Dayton stayed on the line a few seconds more, would she have said something else?

Talk.

There was a chance, however small, that the command referred to a matter other than her job application. Coming from Kenna, 'talk' could've just as easily meant 'explain' in which case he had failed her during their brief call.

Talk.

Though her voice always sounded lyrical to Dayton, he did not miss her falsetto of irritation upon picking up. She'd wanted him to get to the point. Kenna's stilted breathing in the beat of silence before he spoke told another story.

A soft, hollow knock reverberated on the door. Bringing a fist to his lips, he consulted the time. He'd neglected to post his 'out to lunch' sign again.

His 12 o'clock was obnoxiously early.

Reaching for the doorknob, he gloated thinking of the menial tasks he'd dump on Kenna in addition to her administrative work. She may have backed him up against a wall but he had no intention of relinquishing control.

His office, his rules.

The door swung open to reveal a woman with a closed, raised fist, as if ready to knock again. Her shoulders inflated with an inhalation she refused to release.

"I hope I didn't disturb you. There wasn't anyone behind the front desk so I thought I'd check back here before I left. Are you?" Lashes flitting, her eyes traveled the length of him. "Are you Dr. Merino?"

Dayton plastered on a smile.

"I am, and I'm sorry to have kept you waiting. I've hired an office assistant but she isn't due to start until next week, I'm afraid." He led the woman through the hallway and unlocked the door facing the waiting area. "Please, come in and make yourself comfortable, Miss ...?"

"Wells. LaToya Wells."

She indeed made herself comfortable, letting her designer purse drop to the floor and stepping out of her heels. LaToya plopped onto the wood trim velvet couch he'd gotten for pennies at an estate sale. He settled into the chair, nearest the door, and assessed the woman lying across the room.

LaToya. An 'L.' Despite her lean frame, it was easy to discern her strength. Thin, elongated feet. Toned calves. A long neck highlighted by the jet black bob that ended at her jawline.

Not only was she beautiful, but an elegance suffused her presence. This was the one, a fine candidate for his research.

As it stood, Dayton had no interest in carrying on with the

11

sport of seducing women that he shamelessly labeled treatment. Treatment he no longer needed.

He'd found his cure.

And yet it came as a surprise that LaToya had no effect on him. Palms devoid of sweat. Heart never straying from its electrical impulse-induced rhythm.

He swiped his pen and legal pad off the side table.

"What brings you in today, Miss Wells?" His brain shifted from drive to neutral. Evaluation mode.

Bellowing thunder rattled the windows, birthing a dash of lightning in its wake. Rain streamed against the glass in a continuous waterfall. Whatever small joy he used to get out of thunderstorms vanished after the night Kenna spent tangled in his sheets. Every time the sky roared, he thought only of what he'd lost.

LaToya's head lolled to the side and her body jolted as another round of thunder detonated in the darkened sky. She shut her eyes. They reopened, fixed on him, backlit by a fearful desperation.

"I've been seeing my father."

Daddy issues, a conclusion he might have arrived at had she been a Ponderosa student what with the thousands of dollars her attire was worth. However, Dayton had learned since starting his private practice that the issues of real-world adults tended to differ from those of the college students he'd treated for years.

"I see. Do you get along well with your father?"

"We were never very close. He's dead."

Few lines had been exchanged and he could feel the exhaustion waiting for him at the end of Miss Wells' session. Hallucinations were tiresome to treat. He always used medication as a last resort if cognitive behavioral therapy failed.

Maybe he'd jumped the gun and a bit of clarification would relieve the premature burden he felt.

"You said you've seen him. Have you taken to visiting his burial site?"

"No. I see him in my home."

Each of the 60 minutes spent with LaToya was its own prison sentence. Dayton's mind had crashed and was of little use to his patients the remainder of the afternoon.

A deep, tired honk of a horn blared outside the office as he flicked off the lights and gathered his belongings. He locked up before racing through the pouring rain to the idling station wagon.

Carmen, his twin sister, sat behind the wheel, black and gray tattoo sleeve peeking out from the cuff of her coat.

"How was your day?" she teased with exaggerated enthusiasm, pulling away from the curb before Dayton clicked his seatbelt into place.

"Fine."

"Don't act so happy to see me. Please."

He shot her a pointed look that barely contained his annoyance. "Long day, Caramello."

"We'll go out tonight. Make you forget all about it. 'Til tomorrow, anyway." Her winged-liner eyes darted to him and then back to the drenched road. "This weather is something, huh? It's like the sky is falling out. Mom and dad would say—"

"The angels are bowling."

Carmen produced a weak smile. "Yep."

She'd requested leave from United, glad to abandon her mundane flight attendant duties for a couple of weeks, when she concluded through their ritual Sunday evening phone calls that Dayton was depressed.

He was, in fact, not depressed and Carmen would know that had she taken even the most basic psychology course before dropping out of community college.

"By the way," she said, "mom mentioned she'd appreciate a call from you now and then."

"I hope she isn't holding her breath on that one. I think they're still convinced I'm the bad seed."

She laughed and the pitch of her voice rose. "*You're* the bad seed? No, I think the roles have reversed ever since you earned your shiny PhD. And I'm the tattooed daughter from a family of doctors who ran away to Los Angeles, where all the other lost souls collect and decay." Her grip on the wheel tightened. "They have no reason to think that now, do they? They don't know about Audrey, and what they do know about … that was a long time ago. High school. It's in the past. Right? I mean, I haven't gotten a confessional call from you since you moved to this fuck all town. You've changed."

An ache spread through his chest in time with the white flooding her knuckles. Of course, there was a handsome list of misdeeds to which Carmen wasn't privy. He'd committed unspeakable acts.

Some, unforgivable.

"Right," he echoed.

They turned onto the highway and the car struggled in its acceleration to keep up with the hilly, winding road. Water collected in ditches and dripped from pine needles. A deer lay dead at the edge of the pavement, a blotch of red staining its fur, and Dayton looked away. It was too familiar.

The rain. The blood.

"I love you, but honestly? This wagon is a piece of shit. It stalled out on me twice today. I'm sure the balance in your savings account has a comma in it. Maybe it's time to upgrade."

The comment hit Dayton like a sharp slap.

Kenna. Her childish, blue bike. He'd almost forgotten.

"Pencil in a change of plans for the evening."

4

MARKED

Kenna

*A*ugust was the warmest month in Oregon.

Relief was seldom granted by way of shade or a light breeze, but even so there was no escaping the humidity. That silent predator, thickening the air and sticking to skin.

It was how Kenna felt as she set foot on campus the first day of term. She looked out at the buildings, the lawn, the place she had called home for four years. Something had shifted. Or perhaps she was the one who'd changed and she was seeing the university clearly for the first time. Students passing by without hellos and the overgrown ivy on the brick and the third-floor window in Markham Hall, always illuminated with a light unbefitting its dark past.

Tugging on the strap of her bag, she took it all in. She had never heard of graduate school when she'd arrived in Branch Spring, but she'd gone straight to the dorm address her guidance counselor had written down and figured out, day by day, how to function in the real world.

As Kenna idled on the sidewalk leading out of the parking lot, she wasn't sure what was a greater testament to her endurance: the milestone of making it to grad school or besting Dayton at his own twisted game.

Redoing her practicum ruined her summer but it hadn't delayed her studies. She was still on course for the life and career she wanted. That was all she thought about as she breathed in and the heavy air weighed down her lungs.

A gentle breeze wrinkled a flier poorly attached to the nearest lamppost and the motion caught her attention. She stepped closer, drawn in by the smiling girl in the picture. It was fate that she even saw it at all since the staff were swift to take down anything illegally posted to campus property.

Her blood ran cold. The paper announced the time and date of an annual vigil for Bella McAnders, as if God were reminding her that Dayton was bad news.

Quickly, she took a picture of the flier before the click of a car locking ushered her to shove the phone back into her pocket. Liza had insisted on giving her a ride and she'd been too caught up thinking about her impending afternoon with Dayton to refuse.

She approached, all smiles and wide-eyed excitement. For true academics, like both of them, few things were more stimulating than the start of a new term.

"I dropped my phone through the gap between the seat and the console. Took me ages to get it. You weren't waiting for me all this time, were you?"

"Oh no, I was just admiring the view."

"Really? You seem ..." Liza searched her face while reaching for the right word. "Upset."

Was she? Last semester, she spent five days a week in Dayton's office. Now, he was no longer an employee of the university and—while she shouldn't—she felt largely responsible for his resignation. And though she spent every second of break hating him, his absence on campus hurt more than she cared to admit.

The girls fell into step. They wandered along the paved pathway that cut across the lawn and diverged into routes for different buildings. They passed a guy Kenna recognized from her biological psych class last spring and he looked her up and down as if she were a rare cut of meat.

"Welcome back, slut."

Her skin tightened and a cold sweat broke out, chasing away the sheen the humidity had left behind. If Liza heard the remark, she didn't say anything. Not directly.

"I know you said it's all gossip, but that doctor?" Her fingers sailed through her hair, ruining its part. "You don't have to answer, I'm just curious. Did you have feelings for him?"

Everything that connected her to Dayton flashed through her head. Every shard of every broken memory.

"Almost."

Kenna stood at the sink in her bathroom, wiping off the plum lipstick she'd applied for the third time. Her lips looked fuller as a result of the excessive scrubbing. She tossed the tissue into the trash with a deflated huff.

While she had welcomed the morning's familiar chaos of rushing around to classes, that high had settled and terror laced her bones as she regarded herself in the mirror. Dayton was expecting her at his office within the hour.

Getting involved with him a second time defied all logic, but it was almost as if she'd had no choice.

Something within Kenna had compelled her to leave the letter in his dropbox. She suspected, with a powerful certainty, that she had hardly uncovered all he had done.

What she knew about him wasn't enough.

She wanted to dive headlong into the depths of his darkness. Excavate the parts of himself he'd kept hidden.

There was one small oversight in her plan.

His new practice was 15 miles away, which meant biking 30 miles round-trip. Blind rage had precluded her from considering the logistics of transportation to and from East Haven when she delivered her application. Then, she'd taken a cab, but 10 rides per week was far from practical.

Dayton's job posting had quoted an hourly pay that exceeded what she earned at the Nicholson Library, and more still than she'd earned bagging groceries at Roth's while she begrudgingly redid her mentorship. Kenna didn't mind working there. They were, at the very least, oblivious to the sexual politics of the university.

The slight salary bump was just an extra perk.

The real value of the arrangement was all the clinical experience she'd have under her belt—that and whatever new information she could suss out. For someone she knew so much about, it seemed she knew Dayton very little.

Stomach roiling, she stared at her reflection. Her outfit did not stray from her typical style: an off-white peasant top, flared jeans, and ankle boots. The top was sheerer than she liked but the white bra she sported beneath eased some of her discomfort. The bra that, months ago, she'd dug out of the bathroom trash. She hadn't wanted to retrieve it, not exactly, but a manic corner of her brain insisted upon it.

That was the moment she understood that he had left a mark, that she was destined to one day tell fond yet disturbing, tear-filled stories about him like the young women she'd spoken to last semester.

Kenna was one of them. Marked. Marred.

Thoughts running wild, the bra's band seemed to dig into her skin, a lasso tightening around her ribs without mercy.

She hated herself for trying to impress him, for seeking out this job and once again getting tangled up in his web. Most of all, she hated the feelings for him she still harbored, the affection she carried around while overlooking its rotten, decomposing state.

"Stop it," she gritted out.

Her wrist nudged the faucet and she bent forward, splashing cold water on her face. She stared into the drain until her heartbeat felt less erratic and her breathing leveled out.

Migrating to the living room, she grabbed her bag as well as her phone to order an Uber. A notification of a new text halted her opening the app and instead she tapped the message icon. The newest thread rendered her immobile.

> D: You may think I'm cruel, but I'd never hire you unless you had a reliable means of transportation. Check the flowerpot at the bottom of the stairs.

She had an influx of nausea and regretted skipping lunch as the words on the screen stared back at her. Had he been at the apartment complex? When? Was he still there?

Her hands shook as she tried to lock the front door.

As she clomped down the stairs, her gaze did not stray from the potted succulent on the bottom step. It wasn't there when she got home from class. Kenna knelt and snatched the glimmering set of keys lying in the soil. Hand closing around them, she scanned the parking lot but had no trouble spotting the car that didn't belong.

Dayton's station wagon.

The hideous wood side paneling blurred into its beige paint as a wave of disorientation hit.

Moments she had shared with him in that car, pleasant or otherwise, came flooding back and she froze on the spot while her mind flicked through the scenes she'd fought to forget but proved unforgettable.

While she wasn't terribly familiar with cars, she managed to open the driver's door after fiddling with the antiquated key-in-lock business for a few minutes.

She climbed inside and all of her senses became numb, useless, so as not to feel the warmth of the seat or smell the mint cologne lingering in the cabin. The scent cracked Kenna's resolve and it became easier to understand why the other women had romanticized their memories of Dayton to some degree. One pull of the cologne and she felt like she'd taken a hit of the world's purest drug. So what if it left her vision hazy or accelerated her breathing?

But the smell was habit-forming and she knew she needed to cut the cord before an addiction formed.

Tenuous raindrops pelted the windshield. She got out of the station wagon and ordered her ride, eyes misting over as she waited in the rain.

Upon being dropped off in front of the practice, she received a message from Dayton telling her to park around back. Street parking was reserved for patients. Of course, she had not driven, though she walked around the building for curiosity's sake and caught sight of, what she assumed to be, his new car. It was sleek, dark, and sporty.

Somehow, it fit him as well as the Caprice.

A digital bell chimed as Kenna swept through the front door and was met with an uninhabitable, subzero environment. The A/C must have been set to tundra.

The waiting area was modern and minimal. White walls. Metal blinds. There were a pair of gray chairs with wooden frames separated by a small, round, glass table that housed a few magazines.

So far her and Dayton's new dynamic operated strictly on demands and instructions. Settling in behind the check-in desk was no different. A neon sticky note reading 'for my A.A.' adorned a legal pad sheet. He hired her on as his 'administrative assistant' because 'secretary' was apparently too sexist and dated even for a man who fooled around with former patients.

Peeling the note away from the paper, she scanned the lines containing his illegible handwriting.

-Greet patients upon arrival
-Have them fill out the intake form and collect insurance information if they aren't an existing patient
-When you see a patient exit the leftmost door, send in the next
-My lunch hour ends at one, flip the sign on the front door back to 'open' upon your arrival each day

She scurried over to change the sign before reading further. Change the trash. Clean the bathroom. Answer the phone. Schedule and reschedule appointments.

No breaks. According to Dayton, 'four hours of work doesn't warrant a break.'

Finally, she came upon the final request.

-Stay out of my personal affairs

Rather than eyeing the bullet point with any trace of wariness, a thrill bloomed violently beneath her skin. Did attending a vigil for one of his deceased patients count as an infraction of this rule?

The first patient soon arrived and Kenna slipped into her best attempt at professionalism, a hard task with her former mentor turned ex-lover on the other side of those walls.

Dayton appeared before the psychotherapy room and the silence grew taut as she studied him, though nothing had changed. The same scars and overgrown hair and the seductive yet threatening pull of his lips he passed off as a smile.

His dark eyes swept over her. It was the briefest of acknowledgements but it triggered a series of hair-raising images. His hand around her throat, his bedroom, the pictures.

"I'm ready for you, Ms. Castillo."

Malice dripped from his every word, even when his clinical persona was engaged. That sinful voice was a humanized form of aposematism, warning others to stay away.

And she had not listened. She'd wandered straight to the center of his universe; the precise place from which, months earlier, she had narrowly escaped.

The door shut with a snick and Kenna was alone in the reception area, bathing in the fluorescent lights as beads of cold sweat jeweled on the nape of her neck.

5

BELLA

Kenna

The sun hung orange and magnificent in the sky as Kenna skidded to a stop outside of the cemetery.

The wrought iron gates and unkempt landscaping were eerie enough on their own but she imagined their effect was magnified tenfold once it was nightfall.

There was no parking lot. Instead, a one-lane road snaked through the grounds. A literal highway to Hell. She followed it until she came upon a line of cars, tires touching both pavement and grass, and heard a distant voice.

Her heart climbed the walls of her throat as she drew nearer to the source. Kenna kept her distance, standing a couple rows of tombstones away.

A group of no more than 20 people was gathered around one of the graves, all holding unlit candles. One woman buried her face in a man's shoulder and wailed. A teenage boy looked at the tombstone with a blank expression, perhaps staring at the final resting place of the sister he'd hardly known. An elderly woman kissed the knuckles of her thumbs, hands steepled in prayer, as she chanted under her breath.

A man with a thick, dark mustache stood beside the tombstone, holding hands with a woman whose face suggested she'd made crying a full-time job. Bella's parents.

The father spoke. "Tonight marks five years since we lost our Bella. Even though He took her from us too early, she died loving God, just like she loved all of you. Bella had a big heart, and she had no problem opening it up to people. She traded this life to walk with her Lord and Savior, but she'll never truly be gone. We'll remember her, honor her, and love her. Always."

He paused, striking a match and lighting his candle. He tipped the flame toward his wife's candle until the tip went cherry red and its own fire roared to life. She went up to someone in the crowd, using her candle to light theirs, and the process continued until everyone's had been ignited.

"We light these candles as a symbol of keeping Bella's memory alive. Let us pray."

Kenna bowed her head and prayed along with the McAnders family. She didn't know them nor had she known their daughter but they were connected by a thin, vile thread.

Dr. Dayton Merino.

The parents left first, followed by some of the older relatives. One by one, people extinguished their candles and climbed into their cars. A woman wearing a black baseball cap remained. Her hand cupped around the flame, protecting it from the gentle night breeze. She fixated on the grave, just as the McAnders boy had.

The sun sat lower on the horizon. Kenna had a gig downtown. She knew she couldn't stay much longer.

Dead grass crunched beneath her feet as she moved toward the woman. She stopped several feet away, within the stranger's field of vision, and clasped her hands together as if she were there paying her respects to the dead girl rather than exploiting grieving attendees of the vigil.

A pair of puffy eyes peered at Kenna from under the bill of the cap. "How did you know Bella?"

"I didn't." She quickly amended, "We had a mutual friend."

"She was a good person. I thought things would get easier after five years. But the guilt hasn't let up."

"Guilt?"

"We were roommates. Every year, I come here and I see the pain her family's still in, and I think, 'I could've done something.' Maybe if I'd acted, she'd be alive. If I had woken up, or ..." She shook her head, tears falling to the cracked soil.

Kenna studied the tombstone. *Bella Dade McAnders. Beloved daughter and sister. Oct. 12 1994-Aug. 22 2015.*

The date of death carved into the limestone sent a chill down her spine and it didn't take her long to put the pieces together. She'd reviewed the Polaroids so many times their inscriptions were committed to memory.

Bella died three days after she slept with Dayton.

Questions thundered through her head but one demanded attention above the rest.

Were any of the other girls dead?

The sky grew darker overhead. Her pulse echoed in her ears and she lost all interest in showing up to perform at Striker. Kenna wanted to lock herself in her room, draw the curtains, and comb the internet for crumbs of information until she couldn't see straight.

The woman rubbed her eyes and shaky laughter escaped her lips. "Sorry about that. I'm Taylor, by the way."

"Kenna."

"So, you said you and Bella had a mutual friend?"

"Dr. Merino. Do you know him?"

"Only what she told me, but she always called him—"

"Dayton."

"Yeah. She thought he was like the Mick Jagger of psychiatry or something. Really admired the guy. And she definitely had a thing for him."

Taylor hadn't known Bella and Dayton were involved. They must not have been incredibly close roommates.

"I'd like to ask you something," Kenna said, toes curling in her boots. "I don't mean to upset you, but I'd like an honest answer. Do you think Bella jumped off the roof? I mean, purely of her own desire."

"Her parents don't believe it. They're not very rah rah about mental illness, though. Anyone who really knew her knew that she was suffering, that even on the days when she was smiling and functioning, there was something broken in her that none of us could fix. Not even that rock star doctor."

Though the conversation with Taylor had her second-guessing, Kenna decided to play the gig. She needed the distraction, and playing at Striker Lounge would keep her away from her apartment for a few hours. Whenever she did arrive home, she'd resolved to not look at her laptop.

She wouldn't spiral out of control like last time.

She had stayed at the vigil much later than she'd intended and, as a result, she was expected to go on within minutes of her arrival at the bar. Kenna was grateful for the rush as she ensured her guitar was tuned. Otherwise, her mind would've ventured down dark avenues.

Holding up an arm to shield herself from the spotlight, she stepped onto the wooden shipping pallet that served as the stage. Her arm dropped limp at her side once she was behind the microphone. The light shone relentlessly and a sea of expectant eyes were on her. Wooziness overtook her. She gripped the mic, steeling herself against a bout of sickness that never came but the possibility remained. It stayed close. A halo of nausea crowning her head.

"My name is Kenna O'Callaghan. How are we feeling tonight?"

The introduction felt pointless. She'd performed at the lounge nearly every week during her second mentorship. It had been an excellent way to blow off steam and rake in supplemental cash. Striker operated out of a renovated matchstick warehouse. It was a welcome change from the poorly lit, cramped digs at The Rusted Monkey, which was the only other venue she had played in the city.

She got into position to play her first song, lips already parted in anticipation, but movement near the bathroom stole her attention. The sight she was met with chilled her from head to toe.

Bella McAnders, dirt staining her skin, donned in moth-eaten clothes. A pair of flies circled her head. One of them landed on her lower lashline and crawled into an empty eye-socket. A horrifying, slow smile stretched wide across her decimated face and Kenna looked elsewhere before doubling back on the spot where the dead girl stood.

Except when she looked back, there was no girl, just a tall, dark-haired man who ducked around the corner.

Seeing the ghostly apparition of Bella shook her to her core. She'd been prepared to break into something by Fleetwood Mac but instead chose a song that would allow her to process her heightened emotions; a stripped down version of Radiohead's 'Creep.'

The entire time she sang, she wondered if Dayton was there, in the bathroom, listening to her voice reverberating off the tile. It wasn't that she wanted him there. She felt him.

For disquietude followed him wherever he went.

Her head cleared after she played a couple of songs but as she strummed the opening chords of a third, she spotted a familiar sight at the bar and her anxiety unfurled its creeping tendrils once more.

Kenna's fingers were steady on the fretboard and the melody poured in a steady stream from her mouth as she spied the man.

His back was facing her but he was the right size, the right build. The same shaggy, unkempt black hair. But she finished the song and he turned in his seat, clapping along with everyone else.

It wasn't Dayton.

The paranoia had been a result of her overactive imagination, no doubt intensified by spending the evening visiting the grave of someone whose life he'd touched.

And despite the dread coiling around her heart, Kenna prayed he had nothing to do with the claiming of it.

6

WHO IS SHE?

Dayton

*H*e didn't speak to Kenna the first four days she worked under him. Any necessary communication was passed along to her via text.

She never responded, but she did everything that was asked of her without complaint.

Though he had extended her the use of his station wagon, it seemed she hadn't accepted the gesture in full. A different car picked her up and dropped her off every afternoon. Dayton supposed it was a valiant attempt on her end to rile him. Perhaps he deserved that silent condemnation after he'd snuck into her gig at Striker, though her avoidance of the Caprice predated that night. He should not have gone.

It was foolish. No, reckless.

The moment Kenna became his employee, they entered into a dance far more complicated than their initial contract with the university. This arrangement was muddled by more than any

29

ethical consideration or the issue of power dynamics. It was their history that made it so.

He knew the old adage. Those who don't learn from history are doomed to repeat it. Only, he wanted to repeat it, and this time, he'd be ready at every turn to rectify his original mistakes.

Restraint, as much as he could manage, was critical.

When the last patient left at the end of each day, he remained in the session space until he was sure Kenna had gone. It wasn't that he did not want to see her; rather, he was too eager. He wanted, more than anything, to walk out into the reception area veiled in nonchalance, pretending to go unaffected by her angelic face. The one that was emblazoned in his mind over the merciless months they were separated.

With unwavering certainty, Dayton understood that one look at her, one glance, would prove fatal. A split second that would reignite his obsession and seal his fate as a hopeless devotee of a love he didn't deserve yet coveted above all else.

So he remained locked away in the psychotherapy room, minding his patients and for once striving to do the right thing. To leave Kenna alone, to let her live her life, set her free. He was wrong. Their history did not need repeating. It was better off buried deep within the earth. Hidden and forgotten.

But, doing what was right had never been his brand and by the fifth day, he snapped out of the moral high ground kumbaya haze and set out to reclaim what was his.

His forest queen.

He made it a sort of game at first, stealing glances at her as he retreated to his office to file some paperwork. Dayton had nothing to file except the blurry peripheral snapshots of his assistant. The glimpse of denim and linen alluded that she'd not changed the way she dressed.

And the maddening, firespun hair. It was off her shoulders. How it was styled, he did not know. His fleeting peek painted an incomplete picture, one which was intriguing but lacked the finishing details that qualified it a masterpiece. Mona Lisa without her smile.

Her *smile*, there's something he missed.

His 3 o'clock patient rambled about his fear of death, particularly dying alone, to die and to have never known love.

Dayton almost interrupted the session to release the man from his care citing an incident of countertransference until he realized he had not spoken and had merely been listening to Franklin Merrell's eerily similar fears and felt a flush of relief that he hadn't spouted off his own mirrored thoughts.

The patient bid him adieu when the hour expired but he stayed glued to the armchair. His insides quivered at the short, high-pitched beep delivered by the security system as Mr. Merrell vacated the premises.

Though walls kept them apart, they were alone.

Kenna, himself, and 500 square feet.

His hand curled around the door handle. Adrenaline surged through him as he mustered the courage to turn it. The door retreated to reveal his darling stationed dutifully at the reception desk and the romantic, exaggerated opening crescendo of Etta James' 'At Last' swelled in his head.

That is, until Kenna turned her head and fixed him with eyes that used to sparkle like jade but now reflected a dull green, leaves on the brink of fall's fading chlorophyll.

"There's no 4 o'clock today. Mind if I leave early?" Her monotone voice matched her expression.

Had Dayton been totally ousted from her heart? Was there not a low-burning flame of passion roaring back to life when she saw his face?

Brushing off his hurt, he feigned annoyance.

"I pay you until 5, you stay 'til 5."

"Okay."

The computer had already been shut down. A textbook lay open-face on the desk, its pages littered with neon orange sticky notes. Kenna's hand hovered over the bright stack as she scanned the lines. Watching her study reawakened nostalgia of the countless hours they'd spent holed up in his office at Ponderosa. Dayton had been attracted to her quiet inquisitiveness. It was painfully clear she no longer saw him as she once did. Times had changed. Secrets laid bare.

She viewed him as some sort of sexual deviant, no doubt. Her flat gaze suggested as much.

He dared to get closer, squatting beside the desk and resting an elbow on the corner, a threatening foot away from a flinching Kenna. "What is it you're working on?"

"I see the 'stay out of my personal affairs' bullet point doesn't extend to you." Frustration frayed her voice. "Don't act like you care."

"Kenna, I do care."

Her eyes snapped to his flooded with tears, mistrust, and a flicker of anger. "Please, just let me study." She licked her lips, imploring once more, "Please."

Jaw tense, Dayton rose to his full height and resolved to hide out in his office until Carmen notified him she was en route to the practice. He sat inhumanly still in his chair, letting his emotions wash over him one ugly wave after the next. For 45 minutes he stayed like that, breathing in and out and not moving a muscle nor touching any of the files scattered atop his desk. Fury laced his motionless limbs. He'd approached her with a gentleness that bordered on unnatural for him, and even so she put up fierce resistance. That was his folly.

Kenna was never the frightened doe he'd once believed her to be. She was a wise lamb who feared slaughter in whatever form it may take.

Once his sister's message came through, he slipped his crossbody briefcase over his head and reemerged in the waiting room. Her blouse collar hung loose as she dug around in her bag but he didn't stare. He could be chaste on occasion—and, given their previously fraught interaction, it seemed the safest decision.

She wriggled into the straps and crossed her arms. "By the way, thanks for thinking of me and letting me borrow your old car but I don't plan on using it. The whole university already thinks we slept together."

"We did sleep together."

He knew it was the worst thing to say, yet out it went.

"Do you have any idea what it's like for me on campus now? Can you imagine being stuck at a school where every student and professor seems to know you've gone to bed with a faculty member, and all you're trying to do is navigate graduate level courses so you can get your degree and get out?" Hurt fractured her tone as well as his heart. "There's nothing left for me here, you've made sure of that. But here I am. What does that say about me, doctor?" The next words she gritted out through trembling lips, "What's your professional diagnosis?"

Emotions Dayton had never seen her display flashed across her face, draping a curtain of malevolence over her ethereal features. The hard edges she carried from their affair.

He had done this.

His brows gathered in and his mouth opened but he failed to speak. Where could he have possibly begun?

Any ill-fated attempt at offering Kenna an apology was shot as Carmen pulled along the curb in the Taycan.

"Who is she?" she whispered, staring out the window. Then louder, "Who *is* she?"

He felt a pang of guilt. It would've been easy to tell her the truth about Carmen under normal circumstances, but Kenna was one shade of hysteric away from a psych evaluation.

She had no reason to believe anything he said.

"See you Monday, kid."

7
WHAT'S AT STAKE

Kenna

*T*he weekend was nothing short of miserable.

Liza roped her into a comatose-inducing marathon of *The Bachelor*. When the end of each episode came and the too perfect looking bachelor commandeered the rose ceremony, Kenna couldn't help but wonder who Dayton had been courting in her absence.

Her stomach burned as though someone were holding a lighter to her skin. Who was the dark-haired woman in the car and why had the sight inflamed her with jealousy?

This love refused to leave her. She wanted it gone, exorcized, but it persisted with such convincing authority that it must have altered her genetic makeup and become an inseparable part of her.

A pulling sensation in her gut yanked her forth, elbows resting on her knees, as her imagination ran away from her and she transposed the faces of the Polaroid girls with those of the female contestants. Bella McAnders twirled a rose between her fingers, winking at the camera. In this rendering, she was beautiful, restored to exactly how she'd looked in the vigil flier—short, curly brown hair and plump cheeks. And though this hallucination was more attractive than the decomposing body she'd seen at Striker, it was far from pleasant. Kenna shut her eyes.

When she dared to look at the TV again, she saw the generic-looking reality stars. No more dead or discarded girls.

Gradually, her heart came down from its overexcited state. The women grinned from ear to ear before dimming their shine and demurely accepting the single stems. She envied them.

They hadn't fallen for a monster.

"I swear this season gets better with every rewatch." Instead of waiting 10 seconds for autoplay, Liza clicked the button to start the next episode. The recap began and she fixed Kenna with narrowed eyes. "So, I noticed you got a car?"

"I'm not sure if it's mine, technically. It's more of a loan."

Liza quirked a square brow. "Right. Well, I don't know about you, but I'm glad the first week of class is over with. Too much time wasted. How's your new, fancy off-campus job?"

She pasted on a smile though the inquiry inspired her to flee to her bedroom and not emerge until Monday. Every conversation with Liza since she'd asked about her feelings toward Dayton felt like dodging bullets.

"It's going alright, so far."

"Where is it again?"

"A clinic over in East Haven."

She nodded. "Good experience."

In a futile attempt to drown out her guilt, Kenna focused on the mindless show. Sweat collected in her palms as if she'd lied under oath. But she had not lied.

True, Liza wasn't aware of the whole picture, but the glimpse she'd spared hadn't been illusory.

Selectivity and omission were not the same.

Her phone rang and startled both girls. It was facedown on the couch between them and she prayed with everything she had that

Dr. Merino wasn't written across the display. She flipped it over and dread of a different kind took hold. *Home.* It continued its ringing while she held it in her hand and regarded it with a blank stare.

Her father facilitated any and all calls out of their home and she didn't feel like hearing his hoarse smoker's voice, even if it was only for a few seconds as he passed the phone to whoever had requested to dial.

The phone continued to ring.

Frowning, Liza looked at it, at her, and back again.

"Aren't you going to get that? Isn't it your family? What if it's an emergency?"

A pinging notification signaled a new voicemail. Kenna swiped to delete it. Unheard. The operating procedure had worked fine the last year. She didn't have to panic over follow-up texts because her parents didn't believe in the evil that was cell phones. They still had a trusty rotary back on the farm. 'Built to last,' they'd always said.

Kenna tossed her cell onto the coffee table and it landed with a *thunk*. Eyes glued to the television, she mumbled, "Their emergencies stopped being my responsibility a long time ago."

Liza maneuvered into a criss-cross pose on the cushion. "That would never fly in my family. My mom expects a call from me at 7 p.m. on the dot. Every day. Even if I'm out with friends, I have to slip away and give her a call. She's a little overbearing."

"A little?" A corner of Kenna's mouth lifted.

She didn't mind listening to her roommate ramble about her relationship with her family, so long as Liza didn't expect her to do the same.

"All three of us are away at college, so my mom has us on a schedule. After me, my older brother calls at 7:15 and my younger brother at 7:30. Sometimes, we have a group call without her afterward and complain to each other."

"I always wanted a brother." Kenna hadn't realized she whispered it until it was too late.

So much for not sharing anything.

She started braiding her thick mane of hair like they were BFFs mid-sleepover and not two college students who'd entered the mutually beneficial financial agreement of sharing an apartment. "You have sisters, then?"

"Five."

"*Five?* How did your parents survive that?"

"Oh, you know, they just treated us like we were living in *The Virgin Suicides.*"

Liza keeled over with laughter but Kenna's stony expression insisted the comment was devoid of humor. Quiet fell over them and killed the conversation and they refocused their attention on the show.

One of the contestants vented about her jealousy as a result of being excluded from a group date and Kenna channeled that feeling herself, mind retracing its exhausted path back to the woman in the sports car.

The violent resentment she'd felt when Dayton had gotten into the car and it sped off out of sight.

Dayton

Carmen dropped to her knees upon the trail's end, where it opened up to a two-lane highway lined with pines on either side. A fog clung to the treetops amid the gray sky.

It was the same path he and Kenna had run on the 5K.

If he stayed in any one place too long, everything came back to him. Falling to the dirt, all of the strength leaving his body. The helplessness and shame that had wracked him in equal measure. Kenna's lithe figure growing smaller as she sprinted away from him, reducing her fiery ponytail to a blur of color amid the woods' neutrality.

He'd lost track of the number of times he'd revisited the trail, running through the pines and remembering what it was like to have her jogging alongside him. He felt a powerful pull to the sight where they'd coasted within the forest's natural beauty. And now he seemed determined to end his life in the very place she had saved it.

Carmen hadn't known about the incident until after the fact. Dayton returned home to a swarm of concerned voicemails, worried out of her wits that she had not heard from him in days, and was more or less coerced into telling her everything—leaving out the very delicate detail that he owed his life to a student of the university at which he was employed.

Previously employed, at this juncture.

Carmen's hard, labored breathing made him refocus.

"I better be in the best shape of my life when I go back home after what you've put me through. Do you do this shit every day?"

"Every day you're here." She shot him a glare and Dayton smirked into the mouth of his thermos before taking a drink. He replaced the lid and dropped it beside his panting sister. "Hydrate."

He joined her in the damp earth, stretching as she guzzled the water like it was the last of it on the planet. When she finished, a few drops trickled down her chin, wasted. She tried to mimic his stretches but her form was all wrong. Maybe she'd lied about those yoga classes, just another fictional tidbit that she thought made her life more interesting. Evidential proof Los Angeles had gone to her head.

"How are things with Gia?"

"Good. Great. I've been thinking about asking her to move in but I'm never home. Maybe it's pointless."

"You should ask her. If you're passive, she'll slip away."

"You're the last person who should be dishing out relationship advice." She ripped the elastic out of her sweat-drenched hair and it fell around her angular face. "Please tell me you don't run by yourself when I'm not around."

The protective though condescending inquiry was Carmen's way of touting that she was the eldest by three minutes.

"Mind your business." His tone was more flat than demanding.

She seized Dayton's wrist as he flexed his hamstrings and his eyes snapped to her. Her breath still burst in and out, as if she couldn't catch it. "Are you trying to kill yourself? Answer me, honestly."

"I know what I can handle."

"You're a survivor, Dayton. You're strong, but running without a partner? You know what's at stake."

"And you aren't qualified to make any kind of medical judgment," he snapped.

Carmen rose to her feet, arms akimbo as she looked down at her twin. "By the grace of God, you've made it 38 years. It's stupid to put yourself at risk."

He brushed past her toward the Taycan, calling over his shoulder, "If your nagging hasn't killed me, Caramello, I think I'm safe from any cardiac malfunction."

Once Dayton climbed in the car, he checked his phone. No messages. He wanted to reach out to Kenna, call her, send her a text, but he lacked any justifiable reason to do so; unless it was to saddle her with busy work, transcribing analysis notes and the like. He remembered how overworked he'd felt during his first semester of grad school and he decided the brief contact would not be worth dumping extra responsibility on her. Plus, she'd recently aired her disgust toward him. It was best to avoid the temptation of cellular communication and hold out for Monday.

"I caught a peek of your new assistant," Carmen said once they were en route to the house. "She's a pretty little thing."

"Nice try. I'm not biting."

His grip tightened on the wheel. She didn't know anything about Kenna and it was better off that way.

Silence filled the cabin as she gathered her words.

"When I picked you up yesterday you seemed hurt, almost.

That's not like you. It got me thinking, there has to be some kind of history there."

Damn Carmen and her twin telepathy.

"She's my employee. I'm her boss. End of story."

"Here's why that's complete bullshit. You wouldn't let an employee yell at you, and no, I couldn't hear anything so it's not like I have proof, but her whole body shook when she turned toward you and I know I'm not nearly as smart as you but I can read between the fucking lines, brother."

"She and I ..." Dayton kept his eyes on the carless expanse of road. "What we had has run its course."

"Good." The response came as a surprise. Usually, she pressed for details when it came to his love life but now that he had something to report she was playing offense. Almost as if she'd read his mind, she amended, "Look, don't take that the wrong way. If you're hurting, I'm sorry. All I meant is, she seems ... young. A college girl? It could be triggering for you."

"Don't skirt around your words. Say what you mean."

"We don't want a repeat of UCLA."

The mere mention of it summoned unpleasant memories. The cool cinch of handcuffs on his wrists. Audrey dropping to the floor, crying, shouting.

He floored the brake at a four-way stop, jerking them both forward with such force, their seatbelts locked.

"How dare you even insinuate something like that. I'm not the same person, not by miles."

She tried to nod but her body denied her the motion.

Slowly, her attention panned from the glove box and settled upon him. Carmen employed her most haunting look. It was the one she used to get him to see reason. The one that hung around like an angel on his shoulder, staying with him through all of his wretched decisions.

"I really hope that's true."

September

8

GET IN

Kenna

eet me around back once Rogers leaves.
Dayton had slipped the note on the reception desk before ushering Gerald Rogers, a Vietnam veteran, into the session space. The patient was in his mid-70s and retained good cognitive functioning despite the PTSD that made his daily life hell on Earth. Dayton expressed concern about when or if things would progress toward dementia. Technically, Kenna shouldn't have been privy to the details but he frequently asked her to transcribe his analysis notes and, though she had done it perfunctorily at first, it was something she had come to enjoy.

She read the note again.

Meet me around back once Rogers leaves.

Her skin grew clammy as she tried to think of a reason as to why he wanted to see her outside, after hours.

Folding the paper clean in half, she tucked it inside her bag. She shouldn't have been playing this game but it was dangerous, thrilling; and she possessed no will to stop.

Perhaps that was why she was so drawn to him.

Growing up, her life was sheltered and secure. Dayton was the embodiment of everything she was warned of and forbidden from.

Kenna's heartbeat thrummed in every inch of her body as she bid Mr. Rogers adieu and slipped him an appointment reminder card for his next visit. Every system was on high alert.

The computer powered down quicker than usual and she was left with no choice but to collect her things and face the man waiting behind the building. She knew there was a rear exit in Dayton's private office but she would have sooner consumed a vial of cyanide before willingly setting foot in that space. Her hand grew heavy as she pushed on the front door and emerged in the daylight, traipsing along the sidewalk as if she weren't yards away from an incredible mistake.

Fear slithered through her veins and tainted whatever thinly veiled resolve was draped over her heart and mind.

She could've stayed on the sidewalk. Called an Uber. But her feet led her around a corner and then another until she was staring the source of that fear in the eye. No more hiding.

Dayton stood beside his sleek, black car, arms limp at his sides and shoulders squared. Relaxed, in control.

Involuntarily, her gaze swept over his polished dress shoes, tailored slacks, the loose collar of his button-down. The spell was broken as Kenna landed on his stern face with its rippled, pink-white scarring.

"Get in." He held the door open for her, a caustic gentleman.

She stared at the leather seats. A fork in the road.

The shadowy interior of the car undoubtedly represented the path marked 'dead end' but she climbed in, stomach clenching all the while. Wordlessly, he got in the car and soon they were in motion. The radio was off. Not even the engine made a sound as they coasted along the streets and roadways that connected East Haven to Branch Spring.

Anxiety spurted out of her like blood from a slit carotid as the needle on the speedometer ticked just under 90. Once they headed into town and slowed to a tame 50, she found herself capable of speech. The obvious questions came to mind but an unexpected one tumbled forth.

"Why do you see Rogers, no charge?"

Seconds passed and casted doubt on whether Dayton had heard her. He maintained a loose grip on the steering wheel with one careless hand and kept his eyes trained ahead. It reminded Kenna of the day he'd gone with her to Reid's funeral. Her heart still leapt at the memory of him in a suit.

"I had an uncle who fought in the Korean War. Never mind that he survived, it completely destroyed him. My dad told me the stories, how his brother's family fell apart. His wife left with the kids a few years after he'd come back from the war. He got older and some of our relatives chipped in and put him in a nursing home. When I'd go home for the holidays from UCLA, I'd visit him. I didn't tell my parents. No one else visited the guy. He hardly said a word but I told him stories, tried to engage him in something."

His measured voice punctured her lungs and as he spoke she drew no breath. His words became her oxygen, anchoring her to this life.

"Truthfully, I felt this pull toward him. We were both battling something neither of us could control."

Everything she knew about him dulled to unimportance as she parsed out the most revealing thing he'd ever told her. Whatever his affliction was, it was something he couldn't control. A compulsive need. He couldn't help going after the girls. Still, in her mind, it didn't justify his actions.

Nothing did.

But the sliver of information gave her an edge as far as what might have been the guiding force for his behavior.

She ran through the possibilities as they coasted along and, for a moment, some of her fear fell away. Kenna didn't care where they were heading or when they'd return. Her brain was high on deductive reasoning and she was engulfed by the familiar crispness of mint cologne.

One by one, she ticked off the paraphilic disorders. None of them fit Dayton. Voyeurism spared some degree of hope yet it was miles away from what she would have considered a bulletproof diagnosis. Mentally, she turned to the conflicting evidence. The Polaroids were taken without consent but his sexual encounters were consensual. For many people who suffered from the disorder, it consumed them. Their entire life became ruled by fantasies.

From the outside, Dayton appeared sane. He held down a prestigious career, extra shifts at the emergency room. He had hobbies and participated in charity events. He had a family. Friends. He was, by most accounts, normal.

That's what made him so terrifying.

After a pit stop at her apartment complex and one drive riddled with unanswered questions later, they reached their destination: the middle of nowhere.

Or so it seemed.

They were in the station wagon, engine cut, amid a cracked wasteland of asphalt. The Caprice was the only vehicle in sight. Where the pavement ended, the trees began, dotting the lot on all sides. Imprisoned by nature while they idled on the flat expanse of man-made corruption.

Kenna's first instinct was to scream but terror muted her. It sealed her lips and hastened the beating of her heart.

Murder had never truly been something she thought he was capable of, but she could see no other reason as to why he'd brought her to the deserted blacktop.

He spoke right on cue, as if he'd read her thoughts.

"Relax. I didn't bring you out here to kill you."

A violent chill rocked her body but she forced a weak smile, silently praying her discomfort escaped his notice. "Well, why *did* you bring me here?"

Dayton teasingly jingled the keys in front of her face like one might wave a treat before a domesticated animal. Her hand was closed in a tight fist on her thigh but he pried it open and deposited the keys. Flinging open the driver's side door, he motioned to get out of the car but stopped halfway. One foot planted on the asphalt and the other on the floorboard. The corners of his lips lifted in wicked delight.

"It's your lucky day, Miss O'Callaghan. Today, you learn to drive."

She despised the slight knotting of her stomach at hearing *Miss O'Callaghan* roll off his tongue. It transported her to a more fright-ful, though decidedly simpler, time. One in which she studied him rather than experimented with him.

She too barreled out of her respective door and they came face to face as their paths crossed in front of the hood.

"I hope you didn't cancel whatever plans you had for the evening to teach me something so rudimentary."

"If it's so rudimentary, why can't you do it?"

Cool metal dug into her palm as her grip tightened on the keys and she brushed past Dayton. She slammed the door behind her as she ducked into the car and he shot her a questioning look. A look he had no right to dish out, not when he was putting her in this impossible situation.

She shouldn't have been surprised that he'd figured out her secret. He was more intuitive than most but then intuition wasn't required when her range of transportation included a bicycle and ride-hailing.

Kenna siphoned a deep, soothing breath. The keys twinkled in her hand. Winking in the waning sunlight. Wishing her luck. She'd watched him remove them from the metal notch by the wheel moments before but with Dayton beside her in the confined space she wasn't confident she could recreate what he had done.

The parenthetical lines framing his mouth deepened as a frown set in. "You've been behind a wheel, haven't you?"

She stared at it, that circular fixture.

"No. Never."

"Kenna, I've seen your driver's license."

"It's fake. I expected an ounce of common sense from someone who made it through med school and residency."

"I don't understand. Your parents—"

Her head snapped in his direction. "They didn't want us to drive, alright? So they didn't teach us."

"Why?"

His voice was hollow yet brimming with curiosity. Kenna understood how he thirsted for this kind of conversation and how thrilling a moment like this must have been for him. Closer and closer to unraveling the enigma of her existence. And she decided she'd spare him a few crumbs if for no other reason than he still held some kind of sway over her.

Some level of charm she could not ignore.

"They didn't want to make it easy for us to leave."

He slipped into a familiar expression.

It was a face he wore well. The clinical mask he relied upon at the practice. And now it had broken free and found use beyond those four walls. It had penetrated their personal lives, all that existed outside of work and who they were to each other five days a week. Dayton attempted a smile but it was forced and disingenuous and there was no easy transition from the heaviness of what had been said. But he would make it easy for her. He wouldn't say anything further. Not yet.

"The key with the black cap?" He gestured to the set of keys cradled in her half-open hand. "Put it in the ignition." He pointed to the spot to ensure her understanding and there it was again. The rekindling of affection that had been snuffed out months ago. "And twist it all the way to the right."

Her pulse stuttered in her throat as she held the singular key.

Hesitance attacked her on a physiological level until it crescendoed and, all at once, it was too much.

Being trapped in that cabin with Dayton, no one else around for who knew how many miles.

The stirring of buried feelings.

The fact that he was going out of his way to teach her something when showing her the ropes had stopped being his responsibility last semester.

Trembling laced her hand as she slid the key into the ignition but she swallowed the fear, the uncertainty. She twisted it and the decades-old engine sputtered to life. The action was so simplistic and yet Kenna couldn't contain the manic grin that bloomed across her face.

She was a child who'd just taken her first steps and she needed praise, acknowledgment for having figured out something so essential to life.

An emotion she could not pin down swirled in the blackness of his eyes. Sadness? Perhaps, as a result of her overzealous glee, he had realized that she was telling the truth.

"Don't get too excited, kid. We're just getting started."

The clinical mask was gone. The anguish.

All of it vanished. He was unmistakably Dayton. Honey flashed against his dark eyes and his subtle smile crept to life. It was as easygoing as he got and she liked how familiar it was, however unwise it may have been for her to feel that way.

"Alright. Foot on the brake. That's the left pedal." Kenna lined up both of her feet with the pedals but the arrangement was far from comfortable and she was sure she had done something wrong. "And you only want to use your right foot, switching between the pedals whenever necessary."

A red, hot wave of embarrassment might have washed over her had it not been for the patience woven into his gentle tone. It calmed her nerves.

Calm. The last thing she should've been.

"Press down on the brake and, at the same time, maneuver the gear shift from park to drive."

Though she knew next to nothing about driving, she didn't need him to explain that the gears were abbreviated by initial. She managed to shift to 'D' without killing them and kept her foot cemented on the brake, awaiting further instruction.

"Let your foot off the brake."

Dayton gave her a pointed look as she refused to remove her leaden foot. She was terrified about what would happen with things in motion, worried over everything that could go wrong, least of all making a fool of herself.

"You aren't going to hit anyone. In case you haven't noticed, this is an abandoned lot. If you manage to make it all the way to those trees," he pointed into the distance, "then we might have a problem on our hands."

Kenna did not laugh nor remove her foot.

"Where are we?"

"About half a mile from Owens-Adair."

Maybe he hadn't taken her there to teach her to drive but rather to take care of her—she knew too much—and maybe whatever government agency spied on its own people would overhear the location and come to her aid before it was too late. He'd said himself that he had not taken her there to kill her but what if the brash statement was simply meant to throw her off?

Dayton quickly shattered her paranoid, violence-inspired fantasies. "I guess I didn't mention it because I thought it might conjure some memories."

"Good or bad?"

The question was fragile. Paper-thin glass.

"That's for you to decide."

And then he was back to business, as if the brief but intensely intimate tangent of conversation in which they had relived a part of their past had not taken place. His mastery of compartmentalization gave Kenna whiplash.

"Ease off the brake and switch to the gas pedal. Be gentle with it. Light pressure."

The car rolled along the pavement like a giant, mechanized snail and she watched the miles per hour steadily increase in time with the pressure she applied to the pedal, infused with an incredible surge of power as her gentle action propelled the vehicle. 10. 15. 20.

Dayton did not intervene until she clocked 40.

"Let's keep it at 25."

She rolled her eyes but obeyed, slacking off her speed. "I assume the turning is self-explanatory?"

Though he assured her there was no wrong way to turn, after she had completed one from either direction he proceeded to tell her that if she turned like that on the open road, she'd be the source of a pileup and despite the horror of that supposition, laughter erupted from her lungs; because, suddenly, he was the one afraid of being in the car with her.

9

JUST A WAIVER

Kenna

The following week went by without incident. They stayed out of each other's way and Kenna did all that was asked of her. Running to the office supply store across the way when they ran out of printer paper. Cleaning the patient bathroom with a pair of blue nitrile gloves and no hazmat training. She even stayed late one afternoon and helped Dayton brainstorm a new filing system and had been shocked that he kept the whole affair platonic.

Another week passed.

He ducked out early for a cardiology appointment and showed Kenna an ounce of trust when he left her the keys to the practice and told her to lock up.

Their dynamic at the new office was leaps and bounds from what it had been on campus. He didn't offer a greeting upon her arrival or departure. Despite the fact that they had recently opened a second location along their street, there were no surprise lattes from Bigleaf Coffee Company. They no longer shared conjectures about patients because it was his independent practice as a licensed psychiatrist, not an institution of higher learning.

It wasn't that she expected these things.

She missed them. She missed his forced, while trying to be cordial, inclusion of her.

Though, she shouldn't have missed a thing about Dayton Merino, the man she had ventured through the Nine Circles of Hell for in the name of figuring him out and emerged only to discover ...

No, it had not been a dream, and her journey had been far less insightful than Dante's.

Ironically, through all of Kenna's amateur sleuthing and putting her heart on the line, she felt like she didn't understand a single thing about him.

That was impetus enough to keep to herself as she feigned usefulness behind the check-in desk. There she sat, day after day, his pretty little doll on display. The one he used to play with and fuss over. How long would Dayton allow her to remain in the safe confines of her box?

Part of her longed for that day while another part prayed it never came. She'd scarcely put her shattered heart back together after the first brush with his love.

To tempt the same fate twice would forever leave that piece of her unrecognizable.

"Kenna?" Dr. Merino peeked out of the psychotherapy room. His brows were drawn tight, mouth in an expressionless line.

How many times had he called her name?

"Sir?" She despised the formality but defaulted to it when they were in the company of patients.

He shot her a restrained look of amusement.

Clearing his throat, he said, "I asked if you'd like to observe. The patient consented."

Kenna overcame her state of petrification and moments later found herself sitting with Dayton and a woman in her late 30s, in the oppressive 8x8 session space. The discrepancy in scent hit her immediately.

No peppermint oil like his campus office.

Citrus. Overbright and invasive.

She occupied a rolling chair, notebook stationed in her lap, ready to record observations. The contraption on wheels squeaked at the minutest movement, and Kenna felt silly being relegated to the chair while everyone else sat upon proper furniture. A blowtorch grazed her cheeks at the chorus of creaks that arose from it every so often. She was supposed to be a fly on the wall, silent and watchful, not drawing attention to herself. Throughout the hour, her eyes drifted to Dayton as if she were the South Pole and he the North.

An unbreakable attraction bound by an invisible force.

There were wild differences in his posture in the non-academic, clinical setting: legs crossed, an elbow on the armrest as he jotted a string of notes, gunmetal bracelet jostling. Free hand shielding his mouth. His work, no matter the environment, befitted him with a veil of stern concentration.

The next patient wasn't comfortable being observed but the final one of the day consented. Kenna noticed that Dayton's dialogue with the man, Rooks, was oddly minimal. Stranger still, he didn't write a single word on his legal pad. He listened to Rooks and maintained a pensive expression; meanwhile, she had no trouble filling her page with possible symptoms and behaviors of interest. She blanked on a possible diagnosis, but she had plenty of information to sift through and would race to retrieve her DSM-5 once the session let out.

She was poring over her notes when he joined her in the lobby. His coat was left unzipped and his satchel-style briefcase was strapped crossbody.

"Psychosexual?"

"What?"

One hand threaded through her hair while the other gestured in annoyance at her notebook. "Rooks."

They'd been with the man no less than five minutes ago and he seemed to have already blocked it out.

"That much was obvious, yes." Dayton rifled through his bag and pulled out a sheet of paper, laying it beside the notebook. "I meant to have you sign this earlier, but I couldn't, in good conscience, ask you to do so with a patient waiting in the other room."

Conscience. Since when had he acquired one of those?

The pen hovered over the empty signature line. "And what is this, exactly?"

"It's just a waiver, kid. Nothing dangerous. By signing it, you acknowledge that you won't disseminate information overheard or collected from patients to anyone other than myself, et cetera, et cetera. Get the picture?"

She signed and handed it to him, their fingertips brushing in its transference. The touch was brief, inconsequential, and yet the full force of everything she once felt for Dayton resurrected with a jarring urgency. Ghosts of a desire long deceased flickered across his black irises.

Kenna worried they were a reflection of her own.

Dayton

Kenna's distrustful tone upon being asked to sign the waiver had stung, but it was nothing a series of vodka limes couldn't solve. Over the summer, he had drastically cut back on his alcohol intake—at the fervent insistence of his cardiologist.

His willingness to take his well-being seriously had gone out the window since she'd re-entered his life.

"Another?" Sasha arched a judgmental brow and that disbelief spread to the rest of her face. Dayton nodded as she swiped the collection of empty glasses scattered before him, managing to aim a finger despite both of her hands being full of barware. "I'm cutting you off after this one, Merino."

Nathan slapped him on the back and the abruptness of the contact ripped him from the clutches of his subconscious and delivered him unto reality: a weeknight at The Rusted Monkey. He now had a beard, which he kept at a reasonable length, but even so it was unruly and incongruous with his overall look. It was a sign of his marriage taking root. He and Charlaine were together, settled. No need to impress.

"I haven't seen you drink like this in a while," Nathan said, hand curled around his sweating beer. "You better let me drive you home. You don't want to wreck your new Bruce Wayne car, end up like the last one."

Dayton's fingers flew to the swooping scar on his collarbone. Fractured memories of that evening played through his head. The torrents of rain. The day's waning light.

Tyler's car wrapped around the impenetrable trunk of the Western Red Cedar. His own car, totaled and flipped among the slicken banks of grass and forest rot. The musky smell of the air mixed with exhaust and the tang of copper in his mouth. The day that his game of research had gone too far.

Events he'd never be absolved of no matter how often he sought confession.

"Hey, man, I'm sorry. I didn't mean—"

"It's alright," Dayton clipped.

He and Nathan were still getting their footing around each other. His distasteful display at the wedding had spelled disaster for their friendship, but with time and space the rift was mended. When fall classes resumed, he'd texted Dayton and asked to get a drink.

They'd met faithfully every week since.

"So, I have some big news. We're expecting."

The statement dragged along his eardrums like a knife. Grazing but never puncturing the sensitive membrane. He sat dreading a pain that never arrived and yet he was awash with a mix of emotions he was reluctant to claim as his own.

"Parenthood." Dayton said the word slowly. It spread on his tongue like poison. "Congratulations."

Sasha slung a fresh drink to him across the bar. Vodka sloshed over the rim. "That's it buddy."

"Yeah, yeah."

"Got any advice for me?" Nathan asked.

"What advice do you expect me to give? I'm an aging bachelor who's rarely been given a glance of a real relationship. I'm undomesticated. Wild. But you, you're a pedigree, and this father business? You were born and bred for it."

"You really think so?"

"I do."

Nathan drained the rest of his beer and stuffed a wad of singles in the tip jar. His eyes sparkled with amusement behind the lenses of his glasses. "I may have entertained your little look the other way act just now but, you forget, I know you. You're pissed off about something so how about you quit BS'ing me and tell me what's up."

The vodka flowed over his lips. He drank and drank without taking a breath, drowning in the stinging liquid. Dayton slammed the tumbler onto the counter, startling the patrons on either side of them and earning a pointed glare from Sasha as she cashed him out.

"I hired an office assistant."

"That's great, right? You said it's been a logistical nightmare without one, having to juggle everything on your own. So, this begs the question, why aren't you relieved?"

He stared at the melting ice cubes and lime wedge resting in the glass. He couldn't look at Nathan during the deliverance of this truth.

"It's Kenna." More quietly, he repeated, "I hired Kenna."

"Jesus H., Dayton." Nathan went silent for a long moment,

lifting his glasses and shielding his eyes. "Some of the faculty had the nerve to approach me and ask if you guys were still a thing. I guess they remember how chummy you and I were. I don't tell them anything because I don't *know* anything. Among the colorful things you said at my reception, you confided to me, in private, that you loved her." He made steady eye contact, daring him to deny it. "Were you serious?"

"I still have feelings for her."

"Come on, man, she's a kid."

While he often jokingly referred to Kenna as 'kid,' Nathan's more literal meaning struck a nerve.

"Hardly. She's 22 years old."

"And 22 you are not. You were her mentor and now you're her boss. This isn't a morally gray area. It's black and white. Does the phrase power imbalance mean anything to you?"

Tilting his head, he feigned confusion but his face quickly hardened. He had long grown tired of Nathan Jiminy Cricketing his way into the situation with Kenna.

"I don't know. Does the phrase mind your own damn business mean anything to you?"

"I'll drop it. For now." His gaze flicked upward as he dismounted the barstool, gesturing for Dayton to do the same. "Kick your drunk ass into gear and let's split. I have to drop you off at your place and Charlaine will be all over my case if I'm not home by 11."

The mention of his wife turned Dayton's heart to stone. Reflecting on mementos of lovers past no longer brought him satisfaction. A magical alchemy, pure and scarce, of which he'd long been a non-believer had transformed him.

Love.

Only, he hadn't realized he had fallen victim to its alluring properties until it was too late and Kenna had uncovered fractured pieces of his past and fled.

Nathan's wedding band glinting beneath the streetlights—or

perhaps it was his present brain chemical imbalance—reignited flames of passion in the darkest recess of his soul. Bright bursts of memories assailed him.

Her carefree smile behind the wheel of the station wagon. Hair shrouding her face as she hunched over the reception desk. A bobbing foot betraying her restlessness during patient observations. Recently, his life brimmed with these flashes of Kenna. Diaphanous and impossible to grasp.

No matter the obstacles, he would have her.

October

10

PROFESSIONAL

Dayton

*I*t had been the alcohol talking.

He didn't need to reclaim Kenna. No, he needed to stay away from her, to let her rebuild her life and try to do the same for himself. This was where his research was destined to end. No more games. No more heartbreak.

With the state of his health the past year, he couldn't afford to hold onto such emotionally taxing extracurriculars.

A change was needed.

And while he would've preferred resuming his role as the lover, that had not exactly worked out in the past. Instead, he became his version of a perfect gentleman. He equated the self-imposed role to walking around the office with a shock collar latched around his throat.

One false move resulted in pain for both of them.

He only spoke to Kenna when spoken to. He indulged her intellectual thirst on a daily basis, offering the chance to sit in and observe whenever possible, and answering her questions at the end of each day. He even cleared a space in his office for her to stow her belongings so they were no longer relegated to the floor beneath the reception desk.

It was the most trying part of her shift, hearing her boots or Mary Janes or whatever shoe she'd slipped her delicate feet into that morning clack-clacking on the floor as she neared. She swept in with her mint toothpaste and tea tree oil and impressed those scents upon every knob, tile, and screw that comprised his office. Her lush lips curled into something that wasn't quite a smile and she'd offer him a polite goodbye and he would remain in his chair long after she had gone, breathing in the familiar scents and reminiscing on the times she would have stayed. Their university days.

Dayton may have been guilty of peeking at her backside a moment too long when she knelt to retrieve her things each afternoon, but he did not allow the sight to consume him. He didn't comment upon or react to it.

Was this the true meaning of professionalism?

The word he and Kenna had tossed around last semester, a blanket unable to stifle their roaring flames of sexual and academic chemistry.

"Hey, if you're not busy, would you mind coming in here for a minute?" her feathery voice called from the lobby.

He was, in fact, not busy. It was still his lunch hour. She had come in early and the extra time she'd dwell in his presence that day felt like a small karmic gift for striving to be on his best behavior.

He strode along the short hallway that let out into the reception area, soon emerging. "Is there a problem?"

Her attention fell to him like a hot, white spotlight and everything within him hollowed out, leaving him floating in another dimension, one in which he might have gazed into her cartoonish eyes, uninterrupted.

Now they were on him, appraising.

Mascara darkened her auburn lashes and champagne glitter dusted across her eyelids.

Nose wrinkling, Kenna glanced at a sticky note adhered to the corner of the computer monitor. "Mrs. Felvus called and insisted on having her appointment moved up. Hers isn't for another month and a half, but you're booked solid for the next two weeks."

"And did you tell her that?"

"No, I didn't think it was in good taste to deliver bad news over the phone from a psychiatrist's office. I told her I'd consult with you and get back with her this afternoon."

Dayton leaned against the wall, hands slipping inside his pockets. "How professional."

Professional. He'd made peace with that label and yet in spite of his forced gentlemanly behavior it was the last thing he wanted to be. She wore a dress, a form of clothing he had rarely seen her in. Tiny red flowers were printed all over the black fabric. A scooped neckline without showing an excess of skin.

Leave it to Kenna to make modesty seem teasing.

"Thanks?" Her brows pulled in. "What should I tell Mrs. Felvus?"

She crossed her legs and the motion hiked up the skirt of her dress to reveal more of her thigh. His focus was drawn to that smooth expanse, a visual reminder of the night she spent in his bedroom. Those legs had locked around him with startling strength.

A strength he'd long underestimated.

He ignored the dilemma with Mrs. Felvus.

"Special occasion today?"

It wasn't what he wanted to say, but he thought Kenna could do without being hit on in the workplace; especially one in which she had a complicated romantic history with her employer but, god, she was beautiful and he burned to tell her so. He bit his tongue, awaiting her reply.

"Sort of. I had a group presentation in Personality Assessment."

"I miss hearing about your classes."

A hard smile ironed itself onto her face. "Last I checked, bull-shit isn't on the schedule today, Dayton. You don't care one bit about my life."

He stiffened as rage coiled around his ankles, ready to strike. If only she knew.

The problem was that he could not stop caring.

Why else did she suppose he'd hired her? Oh yes, her entirely useless threat of blackmail.

Dayton abandoned his post on the wall, shoulders squared, muscles tense. His jaw ached from its clench. "You'll address me as Dr. Merino while we're in this practice, *Miss O'Callaghan*."

She rose slowly, with purpose, and came up to him. Heat spread within him as Kenna searched his face, lingering on the scar cutting across the hollow of his cheek.

"I don't think so, and if you think you can speak to me in that manner, you're sorely mistaken."

With her this close, the bite of her spewed words and sump-tuous curl of her lips begged Dayton to sin.

Her sweet breath, that gentle fire, swept over his skin. The heat in his core turned blistering and he yearned to pin her to the wall and remind her of what they once had. But he had learned his lesson. He wouldn't scare her away again.

Frames of conflicting emotions reeled across her face.

His open palm cradled the back of Kenna's head and their lips met. To his surprise, hers moved against his. No restraint. Her mouth remained cloistered during the exchange but he did not mind. Excitement hummed through his veins like a narcotic every second she allowed him to feel the soft caress of her lips.

Though she denied him a taste, he smelled the toothpaste on her breath. Tea tree oil. Vanilla. The scents that haunted him in his office and they were resurrected as a part of his life as he threaded his fingers in her hair and silently vowed to never again let her go.

His darling lamb had come home.

He was hardwired on her, tuned out from anything else. The chiming of the security system's digital bell as the door opened escaped his notice.

A voice soon broke them apart.

"Oh, dear. I'll call and reschedule." The woman, who looked as mortified as Dayton felt, turned on her heel and scurried out onto the street.

His lips tingled from their kiss, chest mottled and heart thrashing beneath the trappings of his dress shirt. Kenna had already retreated to the safety of the desk chair.

Ripping the sticky note off the monitor, she mumbled, "A cancellation. It's Mrs. Felvus' lucky day."

"Have dinner with me this weekend."

The proposal halted her mid-dial.

Really, she'd halted for no other reason than to scoff at him, as if she didn't feel it too. The reawakening of this powerful thing between them that laid dormant for months.

Her fingers danced over the buttons and he heard the soft ringing projecting from the receiver. Kenna covered the mouth-piece. "Yes to dinner on one condition, and it's non-negotiable. I want answers. You owe me that much."

11

THOSE GIRLS

Kenna

*W*ith the aid of overzealous prayer and her marginally improved motor skills, Kenna survived her first solo venture on the open road. She began frequenting the abandoned lot after the initial lesson with Dayton. There was something soothing about teaching herself, using his one day of guidance as a mental handbook. When she was behind the wheel, amid all that concrete and the distant army of trees, she felt at peace.

More than that, she felt powerful.

As powerful as she'd felt slipping the letter in Dayton's dropbox, or sneaking out of the farmhouse window at 18 and never looking back.

She breathed a sigh of relief as she parked, feeling thankful to have made it to her destination in one piece.

A few minutes remained before their agreed upon meeting time of 8 o'clock—Kenna had left early so as not to risk being late.

They had never been out like this, just the two of them, outside the shell of their mentorship.

And though it was new and exciting, she couldn't afford to let that excitement shine through.

No dress. No heels. No makeup.

Saturdays were for coursework and her unkempt appearance suggested that she hadn't strayed from tradition.

'Sinclair's' was spelled out in a scrawling cursive neon white sign over the entryway, nestled among a dense network of creeping fig vines. The restaurant screamed special occasion with its black-tie waitstaff and dimly lit, intimate atmosphere.

It was a perfect place for graduation parties. Anniversary dinners. Or, in her case, an elegant backdrop for a dreadful conversation.

The hostess took one look at Kenna's disheveled bun-ponytail hybrid and her brown eyes brimmed with faux sympathy. "Sorry, sweetheart, the bar just filled up."

She kept her face neutral. It would've been too easy to rip into the anonymous girl after the week she'd had. If her thus far limited exposure to psychotherapy had taught her anything, it was empathy.

"I'm meeting someone. I think he had a reservation."

"Last name?"

"Merino."

Her mood changed on a dime.

Clutching a menu to her chest, she leaned over the hostess stand, speaking quietly, "I've been working here for, like, five years and he always dines alone. God, you're lucky. He's way hot."

Kenna might have taken it as a compliment were he a man of upstanding morals. It wasn't a casual evening out. They had unfinished business.

"Back corner booth."

Mumbling her thanks, she rounded the corner into the dining room and with every step she took an image of her semester spent in Markham Hall flashed through her mind. Sitting in that rundown chair for hours, scrawling in her notebooks. Refiling patient folders and running errands.

Fond memories soon gave way to less savory ones.

After hours. Her independent research. The long nights and scarring conversations. And, in the end, she'd been met with the same fate as the rest.

Another photograph.

But at Sinclair's, things would start anew.

No longer was she blinded by her obsession over the wrongs he'd committed. She had reached the bottom, dark and unforgiving, when she had tampered with his box and had spent the summer clawing her way back to the surface.

All of that recovery delivered her to this moment. The shaky edge in her step abated. She was poised, confident.

Restrained contentment backlit Dayton's face as she approached their table. He seemed genuinely happy to see her, as if they were a couple and not a pair of ex-lovers with wildly opposing goals. He rose and placed a hand on her upper arm, craning to kiss her cheek, and she simultaneously loved and loathed how intimately familiar it all felt.

They settled into the booth. Kenna eyed him like he was a puppy who'd pissed all over a brand new rug.

"This isn't a date. Please don't treat it like one."

"Alright."

A green and black flannel and jeans had replaced his office attire. Hiking boots. Dressing down was his version of dressing up for an evening out. Belatedly, she realized it was the same outfit he'd worn when he had cooked dinner for her.

A glass of water sat before him, sweating.

"No vodka?"

"I'm trying to cut back."

"Well, I hope this *leads you not into temptation* but I won't survive the night without a few glasses of wine."

Dayton drank the water but she surmised it was purely as a means of de-escalation. "You're being awfully hostile for someone who negotiated the conditions of this dinner."

"I came here for answers. Cordiality isn't part of the equation." Yanking on the elastic, Kenna freed her hair from its messy presentation. She lowered her voice to a conspiratorial decibel. "And what was that at the practice the other day? You think because I'm speaking to you again as part of a necessary function to perform our jobs that you're somehow allowed to kiss me?"

"You had no problem returning the kiss, darling."

Darling. One word and she was transported to his bed, pinned to the mattress, thunder echoing in her head.

The waiter materialized and reduced them to second-graders squabbling in the middle of an upscale restaurant. Through her embarrassment, Kenna ordered a bottle of red wine.

Perhaps not a wise choice given it was her first outing behind the wheel of a car but the environment in that booth breeded the necessity of alcohol. She didn't wait for the wine's arrival to dive into her questions.

She had courage all her own.

"Care to explain your collection of, how should I put this, erotic photographs?"

Not a trace of amusement graced his features.

"Keep your voice down."

Whether it was fear or shame, the origin of his response did not matter; the fact that she had roused some kind of reaction gave her a sliver of satisfaction.

Saliva, thick and immovable, built up in her throat. Maybe she was in need of the wine. "Who are those girls, Dayton? Patients? Tell me the truth."

It was painful to beg for a truth she already understood.

"Everyone. All except you and—"

"Charlee, I know," she reminded softly.

The sight of the wine in the ice bucket being delivered to the table made Kenna ill. She recounted the Skype call with Charlee, the night she had uncovered the remarkable lingering effect Dayton left on the ones he loved; and like a dark curse it was destined to trail the women the rest of their lives.

She did not object when Dayton seized the bottle of malbec and poured her a generous glass. As if she were a sommelier, she swirled the wine, watching intently as it sloshed against the glass while cogitating on what to say.

"Is this recreational for you? A kind of sport? Some guys—normal guys, one might argue—like the feel of a hefty rifle in their hands. They take that rifle out into the woods and bam. They shoot a rabbit, a deer. Some of them, maybe the ones who are slightly departed from our societal perception of what is 'normal,' will take the animal to someone. Have it cleaned, stuffed, preserved. You're not a killer, not to my knowledge, but like those hunters, you take something from these girls that they can't get back. Something intangible yet horrifyingly profound. I guess I should be counting my lucky stars that you don't have their heads mounted on your wall."

"The names, the alphabetization. Why?"

It was something that had disturbed and stumped her in equal measure and his lengthy pause told her everything she needed to know. Whatever answer he gave would not reflect the truth.

"I know how it comes across. This isn't some deeply layered thing for you to look into. In the past, I've been reckless, and I knew when I was hired at the university I needed to exercise caution. As far as the organization goes—" A line formed at one corner of his mouth, revealing nothing more than his brief deliberation. "It was a way of indulging without overindulging."

"Is that all I was to you? An indulgence?" She hated the weakness invading her tone yet could not disguise it. "Don't answer that."

She couldn't even hide the hurt from herself as her heart compressed to fatal dimensions. More than anything, she wanted to believe the guilt and grief plastered on Dayton's face, but an irrefutable truth cut that hope down to size.

Nothing would ever fully restore her trust in him.

"Did you kill Bella McAnders?" It came out as a whisper, the ugliest word uttered the softest.

"You think because I fucked her, I killed her?"

"Oh, and she just happened to die three days after you slept together?"

"Bella was sick. She died by suicide."

"You were her doctor. You were supposed to *help* her."

"I can't help those who don't want to be helped. She chose to end her sessions with me, against my advice. I think she'd made up her mind about ending her life long before she walked into my office."

The waiter returned and though she insisted she'd lost her appetite, Dayton ordered for her anyway, raving under his breath about how much he adored the rabbit liver parfait.

She thought he was joking until a plate was set before them with grilled slices of baguette and a small jar of what, at first glance, appeared to be a sauce, darkened caramel in color, but she knew it was the grotesque 'parfait,' as he'd put it.

He slid closer to her in the booth and she made no bid to distance herself from him. His cologne saturated the air and she was pleased to note the usual underlying trace of marijuana was absent. Propping an elbow on the table, his fingers sank into his near shoulder-length hair. Dayton was masterful in his attentiveness, void of expression as he stared at her, exuding only patience. Her insides vibrated at having him near but it killed her to focus on his face so she zeroed in on the water.

The absence of alcohol in his cup reawakened a troubling duplicity: her capacity to both despise and be concerned for him.

He spoke, low and gentle. Just for her.

"I want to stand by my promise. Whatever questions you have, I'll answer them as best as I can."

As much as she wanted to dissect the meaning behind the statement, she refrained from doing so. "Does your sudden aversion to vodka have anything to do with your cardiology appointment?"

"Not exactly. My doctor has always advised that I abstain from drinking but I also have a long history of being a disobedient patient. Until recently, I didn't have a reason to care."

She inferred she was the reason and every bit of color promptly fled her face, leaving her with an uncomely complexion. Her mind was all over the place. Fragments of thoughts scattered like a sea of broken glass.

Intoxication precluded her from focusing on his answer long before moving on to the next question. "Your scars, did you really get them from a car accident?"

"Yes."

"When I first came to you with my mentorship, why did you turn me away?"

"I sent you away because I knew you'd be back." His insidious eyes burned with honesty and he held her there in those black pools. "It set a precedent. I didn't want things to be easy between us."

She became hyperaware of the blood coursing through her veins. That warm stream of vitality. She had been a target to him from day one. How did he view her now, she wondered, a loose end?

"Who was that woman driving your car?"

The laugh that escaped his lips took her by surprise. "That would be Carmen."

"And you find this funny, why?"

"She's my twin."

Kenna buried her face in her hands and released a laugh of her own. She felt freer, lighter—or perhaps that was thanks to a third glass of wine. It may have been wrong to share laughter with someone who had caused her great pain, but her intuition advocated for this easygoing aura she and Dayton had stumbled into.

Between the ramping up responsibility of grad school and the constant reminder via ignored phone calls that she had a family 2,000 odd miles away, she rarely had the chance to let loose.

And though her company was questionable, she was presently talking. Breathing. Existing.

Any further questions Kenna had for him were forgotten as he slathered rabbit liver on a slice of bread and playfully attempted to feed her. She turned her head a number of times, dodging the foul food, but finally acquiesced and tried it, wanting to please him in her drunken state. She thought he was baiting her for a kiss. He did no such thing.

Rather, he peered at her intently.

"That wasn't so bad, was it?"

They ate their dinner and had what was perhaps their first pleasant conversation. He told her all about getting the practice off the ground when it first opened, and how he'd used his connections within the emergency room to get patient referrals. She listened, rapt, and waited for appropriate pockets to fill him in on what she was studying, trying whenever she could to connect those tidbits to his ambiguous anecdotes about his cases.

"Would you like to come home with me?" Dayton's gaze flicked to her as he poured the last of the malbec into her glass. "I don't mean any harm. I've enjoyed our conversation this evening and," he paused, Adam's apple bobbing, "I've missed your company."

With a meal and a bottle of wine in her system, and a false sense of safety created by the dinner, she eschewed their sordid past without batting an eye.

"That would be lovely."

12

NO MONSTERS

Kenna

*V*icious pangs shot through her head.

Dizzy and bleary-eyed, Kenna adjusted to the light streaming in through the sheer curtains and highlighting the juniper walls. The cool, calm color had the opposite effect while she studied her surroundings. Full-length mirror. Mahogany dresser. The gallery wall of the same boy and girl.

She's my twin.

Panic set in as she registered where she was and who she'd been with the night before, though her memories did not click into place to form a clear picture.

There were gaps missing, an alarming byproduct of her heedless alcohol consumption, and she paid the price: waking up hungover in Dayton's bed.

Fear controlled her gross motor movements, hands flying to her torso, her legs. A weighted sigh of relief passed over her lips upon finding yesterday's clothes sheathing her body. Being fully clothed was one less thing to worry about. The right side of the bed was made, comforter neatly turned down and the excess tucked beneath the mattress.

She'd slept alone.

Yet knowing that didn't matter. Nothing could've comforted her in Dayton's house of terrors; the place her lust-eclipsed illusion of him had been shattered.

The stillness of the room amplified the thunderous beating of her heart. Kenna drew in a deep breath and leaned over the bed, daring to peek at the space underneath.

Dust-covered floorboards. No box.

"No monsters under the bed."

The voice startled her. She nearly lost her balance and tumbled to the hardwood. Once her heart slid down from the base of her throat, she turned her attention to the doorway, where Dayton stood. He was clad in running attire and muddied tennis shoes, holding two to-go cups from Bigleaf. Sweat bonded strands of hair to his flushed face.

Sitting on the foot of the bed, he extended one of the drinks toward her. "You slept late."

The mere sight of the coffee shop's logo, a silhouette of a maple leaf with scrawling cursive text, injected an ardor straight into her veins that had her cheeks flushing. It made her nostalgic for their mentorship hours. She recalled her genuine surprise the first time he'd brought her a coffee, days after he had attended her open mic performance and taken her out for drinks. Looking back, it all felt so far away when in reality only months had passed.

Kenna resolved not to dwell on that while in his home.

She drew her knees up to her chest and sipped the foam of the hazelnut latte. "You're no stranger to a hangover, I'm sure."

"Smooth deflection."

Quietly nursing her coffee, she watched him unlace his shoes and then use his heel to slide them under the bed. His movements channeled the sluggishness of someone who'd reached the end of an exhausting day rather than someone who'd just returned from a morning jog. Putting his decaf Americano on the floor, he hung his head between his legs and Kenna feared he was seconds away from succumbing to a vomiting spell.

"Hey, are you alright?"

Voicing her concern for him had been normal once upon a time, but now it was like pulling teeth.

It was funny, really, fretting over being appropriate when they'd never come close to fitting the bill.

A low sound of assurance rumbled in his throat. She studied Dayton's folded form and winced as she was struck with the realization that no one was usually there to preside over such a scene. Straightening, he shot her a ghost of a smile. She felt compelled to sustain the trace of cheer.

"It's too quiet around here. You need a dog."

"I hate animals. They piss on everything and leave clumps of their hair everywhere."

"Funny. That's the same reason I don't have a boyfriend."

His lips parted into a magnificent, toothy grin and in that split second he possessed the terrifyingly charming charisma of Bundy.

Minus the violent offenses.

The longer she stayed in the bed, the easier it became to stitch together the fractured scenes from that early day in May when, within a period of 12 hours, they had at last come together and then were irreparably torn apart.

Not quite irreparable. She'd found herself in his bedroom once again, after all. What did that say about her?

As much as Kenna would've liked to pin the whole of the blame on alcohol, she knew that a small part of her had desired this; that she craved to return to the space where she'd never felt more alive.

A depth of feeling she failed to hide cracked her speech. "We never had our weekend. The one we talked about."

Over dinner, he had more or less admitted that she'd been a target from the moment he laid eyes on her and there she was blathering on about their toxic romance as if it had been something real. No wonder he had targeted her. In that moment, it was obvious she wasn't as strong as she'd believed herself to be. It had been easy to forge a cold exterior day by day at the practice but over the course of one evening she had reverted to the way she'd felt in the spring. She found it shocking and irritating in equal measure that those feelings were exhumed with so little difficulty. Though, Kenna never truly wanted to bury them.

Dayton transitioned to lay on his side on the end of the bed, head propped against one hand while he held his drink in the other. "I'm sorry."

The apology was given without a thought but she could tell he had to fight himself over the rest.

"I know I'll never do enough to make up for everything you've heard, everything you've seen." His dark brows gathered in, gaze falling to the comforter. "The things I've done can't be erased."

His eyes burned holes into the blanket and her heart beat with such urgency it was primed to spring from the prison of her chest. They were having a conversation as if they'd been in a relationship for years but that was merely the effect he had on her brain. His presence was as seductive as a binaural beat and left her with the same placebic high.

He opened his mouth and closed it again, as if he'd thought better of speaking. It didn't last.

"You brought out something so foreign in me. It was terrifying and wonderful. Part of me was relieved when you left that day, because I didn't have to tell you that ..."

Kenna wanted to tell him to go on but her tongue grew leaden and an emptiness spread in her stomach.

"I'm in love with you," he spoke softly, sounding ashamed of the confession.

Everything within her stilled.

It had been the last thing she'd expected to feel on her quest to decode Dayton and yet there was no denying she had felt it too.

Not love, per se, but something that held the potential to transform into it.

An affection that had blossomed like a feral rose in a desolate winter garden, beautiful and out of place.

Dayton

A dagger twisted deeper into his gut with every second that ticked on in silence. Dayton didn't expect her to mirror his feelings but he expected her to, at the very least, say *something*.

This was the kind of dance he despised.

The showing of the underbelly. It was why he preferred the catch and release nature of his treatment plan. Intimacy sans the attachment. Once he'd opened himself up to Kenna it seemed he had not been able to stop feeling.

Allowing oneself to be emotionally vulnerable with another person proved to be a more exposing act than casual sex.

Unable to await her answer any longer, he crept off the bed and discarded his half-empty cup on the dresser, where he swiped a clean outfit. He migrated toward the bathroom while she headed for the adjacent doorway that opened up to the rest of the house.

"I'm going to shower. Will you be here when I get out?"

"You drove me here. That doesn't leave me much of a choice, does it?"

"We can go get the Caprice."

Kenna beheld him with her burning gaze and he studied her with an intensity that she quite possibly found offensive, but, every time she looked at him, he feared it may be the last. And so he cataloged every crease, curve, and dimple, not willing to forget all of the little details that made her who she was. His saint, his saving grace.

Beyond the walls, the seasons may have been changing and it didn't matter. All that mattered was in that room. The wicked tenderness of her face.

So this was love, both frightening and thrilling.

"If you want me here, I'll stay." She raised her cup a hair as she turned to leave the room. "Thanks for the coffee, by the way."

A chill wreathed his spine in time with his bare feet meeting the ceramic tile in the bathroom. Each cell in his body was on high alert. He felt himself harden and instinctively spun the cold dial in the shower, leaving the hot one untouched. After peeling off his sweat-soaked clothes, he stepped into the icy stream of water. Being submersed in the biting cold did little to dissuade his arousal.

Idle hands, they say.

Instead of wrapping around himself, he reached for the shampoo. Dayton decided it was unwise to indulge in lewd activity with Kenna over. He'd already dumped an unwanted profession of love on her; if she heard him masturbating through the drywall, she'd probably transfer universities and take on a new identity.

Though it pained him, he kept the shower chaste and threw on his clothes without ceremony. He ran his fingers through his hair a few times, flicked the lightswitch, and wandered through the poor excuse for a hallway that let out into the living room. An inexplicable warmth bloomed in his sternum at the sight of Kenna nestled on his garage sale sofa. He kept a blanket draped along the top of it to disguise the fine rips in the leather which she had repurposed as a cloak.

A forced smile spread on her lips. The action was mechanical, the antithesis of her searing stare in the bedroom.

Perhaps she deemed politeness the safest form of expression to display toward him. The forced nature of it all had Dayton gritting his teeth as his feet carried him to the kitchen rather than the vacant space on the couch he was dying to occupy. Was this how their interactions were forever destined to be, weighted by the past?

His hands shook as he filled the kettle in the sink and was

pierced with a possibility more formidable than Kenna never trusting him again.

A part of her may always fear him.

He put the kettle on to boil and, without reservation or permission, joined her on the couch. They'd sat in the same spot hours earlier when alcohol danced through her bloodstream and inhibitions were but an empty, hollow thing. Scratchy and suffocating silence hung between them. A noose for two.

Kenna pointed out his green and yellow shirt. "The Ducks, huh? Where's your loyalty to UCLA?"

"Are you afraid of me?"

The inquiry was harsh, even to his own ears.

Her eyes darted from him to her lap. A tangle of words spilled from her lips as she half rose. "I should go, really. I have a paper due for Rothman."

His hands shot forth and covered Kenna's thighs, keeping her in place. The thudding of his heart intensified as her pupils grew three sizes, ballooning with terror.

"Answer the question." Her lips were a flat line as he peered into her eyes. If she refused to speak, he had no problem coaxing the truth out of her. Dayton seized a strand of her limp, red hair and slowly coiled it around his finger. "You've looked at those pictures on your phone until you're drunk on 'what ifs' and it's led you to believe that I've hurt some of those girls. I must have, right? Tell me, how far does it go in your mind? Do you think an unlucky few were hacked to pieces? Do you think I have their organs pickling in jars below the floorboards?" His voice quavered with thinly bottled rage. "Make no mistake, Kenna, I've done horrible things. Things that I regret beyond your wildest dreams. I'm a sinner, but I'm not a monster."

"I'm not afraid of you." Chin trembling, her fingers laced with his atop her legs. "But my attachment to you scares me. How much I still care for you, how much I need you."

"And you're scared of that attachment because, to some degree, you *are* afraid of me?"

Her eyes settled on the sliver of space between them, the waxy brown leather. The kettle squealed but Dayton didn't move a muscle.

"The only thing I'm afraid of is your capacity to hurt me, and knowing that when you move on from me, you'll hurt others."

"Like in the past?"

"I didn't say that."

"It's what you implied."

She pulled her hands away and sunk into the corner of the couch. "Interesting you didn't link my flighty behavior to what you said in your bedroom. What right do you have, saying something like that after everything you've put me through?"

Anything that sounded halfway decent to say died long before it reached his tongue. He had no right but it hadn't stopped him from confessing a truth that had burned within him for months. In his desperation to get it out in the open he had failed to consider how Kenna may react to it.

Whether she ran or stayed by his side, the truth would be out. That's what had driven him to act. Sitting beside her now, that logic seemed misguided.

Her voice tore him from his subconscious.

"I don't know what love is. I don't know what it feels like. But, for what it's worth, when I'm with you ... even knowing about your past, you're the only person I've ever felt truly safe around."

Kenna

Her hands clenched at her sides until her nails bit into her palms. It was not until she realized this caused her a great deal of pain did she relax.

Dayton must have thought she'd gone mad, admitting that a part of her feared him while she also felt safe in his presence. She wouldn't have blamed him for thinking it, especially when she thought the same.

The faint ridges on his forehead deepened. "Is that true?"

"I have no reason to lie."

He stared at Kenna, hard and searching. "Do you really have a paper due for Rothman?"

Heat flooded her cheeks.

"Well, it isn't due for another two weeks."

Saying nothing further, Dayton padded into the kitchen and poured himself a mug of tea. He offered to make her a cup but she quietly refused. The clanking of the spoon calmed her.

"If you feel so inclined to work on it, you can use my laptop. It's on the desk over in the corner. Unless you'd rather go, of course."

She stood halfway between the couch and the desk, eyeing him from across the expanse of room. "I meant what I said before. If you want me here, I'll stay."

He held his tea, standing impossibly still in his sweatpants and t-shirt, wet hair framing his face.

"You know what I want."

Did she know? Those words felt like the sharp, cold edge of a switchblade flush against her throat. Kenna didn't feel the slightest degree of relief until she populated the desk chair, alone with her racing pulse and uneven breathing.

Alone as she could be with him 12 feet away.

She didn't want to work on her paper, not really. But the manner in which she had fled to the desk dissuaded her from leaving the chair. She shouldn't have been in that house but she was. Dayton shouldn't have been telling her he loved her and bringing her lattes but he was. They'd gone from a somewhat hostile dinner to her waking up in his bed alone and the infuriating absence of the time in between feasted on her nerves as the computer booted up.

Eyes glued to the keyboard, she asked, "What happened last night, when we came back here?"

"Believe it or not, seeing you clinging to consciousness isn't attractive to me. You talked yourself to sleep on the couch and then I carried you to my room. I slept out here. That's it."

Kenna hooked her arm on the back of the chair, which wasn't an office chair but a dining chair, and shifted her body 90 degrees so that she faced him. "You took pictures of me, asleep, in my underwear. What am I supposed to think?"

He didn't comment but cast her a flicker of a sidelong glance. For a moment, Dayton looked like a normal guy, sprawled on the couch with his collegiate shirt and pregame coverage on the television. But in place of a beer he held a mug of tea and the broadcast was muted and even in that fleeting, still frame, something about him was decidedly off.

The home screen loaded on the laptop and she found it odd that it wasn't password protected, what with his endless supply of secrets.

There were four labeled folders: taxes, residency, practice, ponderosa. She felt a deep sense of gratification upon discovering he had kept a digital record of his university patients. The whole time, she'd been convinced he conducted his clinical work completely offline.

His cell phone rang and ripped through the heavy silence. "Hello?" Scrubbing a hand across his face, he said, "This is he."

Her eyes wandered to the contents atop the desk, confident he was too caught up with the phone call and football to notice that she had yet to open a browser tab.

"Yes, she is."

The surface was littered with the most mundane things but knowing they belonged to Dayton piqued her interest. There was a tiny box brimming with receipts. She didn't flip through them because the rustling paper may have diverted his attention. The topmost one was from a home improvement store, and appeared to be for nothing more than bags and bags of gardening soil. Expression slack, she replaced the lid.

"20 milligrams of olanzapine. That's daily."

In another corner lay a haphazard pile of bills, most of which were medical. Owens-Adair Hospital. East Haven Cardiology.

He pushed to a sitting position, palm flat against his forehead. "No, I've never prescribed lamotrigine." A pause. "You've spoken with the family?"

She dared to slide open the right-hand drawer. Though it looked as if it would produce a horrendous creak, it remained silent on its tracks. A glint of light illuminated a photo within that halted her heart for a beat before it quickened and her throat grew thick. It was of herself, taken when they'd gone to the café in Portland following Reid's funeral. In it, her gaze was downcast as she reached for a paper cup, her mouth agape. Kenna had no recollection of the picture being taken but she remembered he had stepped away to answer a call.

The shot wasn't crisp like his Polaroids.

It was out of focus. Blurred by her movement. There was something charming about the incomplete, in-motion glimpse of her being enough for him.

The discovery should have filled her with outrage but only tenderness washed over her as she looked at the photograph that had been carefully tucked away in the drawer.

Slowly, she pushed it closed.

"The minute she's one iota of coherent, give me a call and I'll head up there."

Abandoning the safety of the desk, she nestled on the arm of the couch, maintaining a respectable and observable distance from Dayton.

"Mania?" she asked.

"You've always been an exceptional student. It's tragic your intellect is doomed to waste away in general therapy."

Tears welled behind her eyes. "I had a good mentor."

13

GOD'S WRENCH

Dayton

*D*ayton thought he'd died and gone to Hell when Kenna quietly asked if she could accompany him to check on his patient who was recovering from a manic episode.

The silent ride to Owens-Adair did not phase him. Her nearness filled the gaps in the absence of her words and, while she never broke the barrier of speech, she hummed a lovely rendition of Adele's 'Hello' alongside the radio. Hearing the muted melody made him ache for the full range of her holy voice. Every note, every intonation brought him closer to God. He was grateful for the humming. For him, it signified hope.

She had not lost all faith in him.

The view on the way to the hospital almost rivaled the beauty of his passenger. Warm colors flooded the forest. Burgundy. Marigold. Ginger. The only green that remained were the pine needles. His eyes continuously flicked to either side of the road, singling out the lush trees that were in defiance of autumnal norms. He had a lot in common with those pines. Both of them were stuck, unchanging. But he had Kenna.

He'd professed his love to her and soon he would have his own seasonal transformation. Shed everything dead from the inside out in anticipation of new growth. Whatever change was necessary to be the man she deserved.

She was disappointed but respectful when he told her she had to wait in the lobby. Afterwards, he drove her to Sinclair's and they idled by the station wagon for an eternity. Neither of them wanted to say goodbye.

They didn't hug. It didn't suit them.

His toes curled in his shoes as the sunlight played off her emerald eyes, crinkling around the edges, and her gaze softened on him.

"See you tomorrow," she said.

Dayton stood there even after she peeled onto the main road, drunk on this strange feeling between them and thankful for the bottle of wine that had sent her home with him.

That was almost a week ago.

Most days, he left a hazelnut latte on her desk before she arrived at the office. He pushed for more observation time and stayed later to take over her light janitorial duties.

Anything with the aim of making her happy.

He extended another dinner invitation and though she declined—she really *did* have to work on her paper for Rothman—he kept at it. In time, he was confident she would soften, reciprocate his feelings, even, and he prayed their love would be enough to wash away every misguided thing he had done.

Or, at least, that's what Dayton had convinced himself of until Friday rolled around and a familiar, distressed face peered into the windows of his practice.

God's wrench in his happily ever after.

Kenna

85

Driving the station wagon to campus was scandalizing.

Some girls would've gotten off on showing up to their university in their forbidden lover's car but Kenna had the opposite reaction. She pocketed the keys, walked along the sidewalk, and prayed no one remembered what car *Dr. Merino* used to drive.

She thought her days would be lived in fear knowing that Dayton loved her. Instead, it made the ever-circulating rumors about them easier to bear. A lightness effused from her. It was exactly what she needed after last semester.

A new chapter, an opportunity to forget all of the heavy things she had seen and heard, even if it was with the man who'd been responsible for those things.

Overhead, gray clouds moved in and darkened the sky. Kenna walked at a more brisk pace as fat raindrops splattered on her clothes and clung to her lashes. She made it to Duniway Hall before it turned into a full-on downpour.

Just inside the double doors, there were a couple of girls passing out papers who weathered a storm of a different kind, and with their red-capped noses and swollen eyes, they were doing precious little to hide it. One of them handed Kenna a flier, saying meekly, "Our sister is missing. Call the number at the bottom if you see anything."

She saw their sorority sweatshirts and understood they had not meant their literal sister. Though she stayed far away from the barbarism that was campus Greek life—thanks to Reid—she knew familial-type bonds were common among those social circles. She felt for them.

"Of course. I hope you find her."

The girl who'd handed her the flier gave a weak smile that sent tears surging into her tired eyes.

Heading toward the staircase, she glanced at the photo and the young woman staring back at her stopped Kenna dead in her tracks.

· · ·

Coincidence.

She chanted it over and over in her head throughout her classes as if it were a prayer. The flier was too horrific to be anything but.

Lacey Greene.

5'5". Brunette. Brown eyes. 21 years old. A junior at Ponderosa and member of Phi Sigma Sigma.

Missing person.

Those bold letters printed across the header of the page incited an intense fear within Kenna, one that liquified her bones and ate through her muscles.

She was missing, not dead.

The distinction should've allowed for a small light of hope to remain flickering in her mind. It was pitch black. Even she could not find her way around. Nonsensical ideas leaped out at her. Illogical connections.

The knob on Dayton's office door squeaked and she crumpled the paper, tossing it into the wastebasket beneath the desk in time with his appearance in the lobby. She smiled uneasily but it was useless.

He had seen her.

She waited with bated breath for him to retrieve the flier. He didn't have to fish around for it. It was the lone sheet of paper in the bin, a detail that would've been useful to her before she'd panicked and hidden it.

Unfurling the flier, his face fell.

"You couldn't get any more coincidental." He eyed her with contrived curiosity. "Where did you get this?"

Appointments were slow that day.

Where was everyone? No one was penciled in for 3 o'clock and yet she wished someone would walk in and save her from his question. Beyond the windows, the street was empty.

Cold sweat jeweled on the nape of her neck. "Campus. Her sorority sisters were passing them out. Posting them everywhere."

Dayton shook his head.

"This is no good." The words sounded odd given the severity of the situation, like an improper reaction to a cancer diagnosis. He discarded the flier once more. "It's equally inspiring and heart-breaking, don't you think? The amount of effort people put in to keep some shred of hope alive." His hollow, indifferent gaze met hers. "The missing rarely turn up alive."

14

SECURE THE PREMISES

Dayton

*T*hursday night trivia was a fixture in his week.

It was something Dayton always looked forward to but that evening his mood was above par.

The wrench had been dealt with, and though Kenna was undeniably distraught about the Greene girl's disappearance, she was still speaking to him.

Halloween was fast approaching and some people appeared to be celebrating early, donned in costumes. No doubt attending parties and the like.

Donovan's *Season of the Witch* blared through the speakers between questions. Dayton looked at the gummy eyeball floating in his vodka and smiled to himself.

Tonight was a good night. He was happy, free, relaxed. Things he hadn't felt since God knew when.

Mind wandering, he considered bringing some of the Halloween cheer to Kenna. He wanted to text her and ask her to spend the night. They'd rent a horror film and he would pop candy corn into her sweet mouth. He would hold her in his arms, reeling in ecstasy whenever she buried her face in his chest to escape whatever chilling image was on the screen.

But Kenna had class tomorrow and he had to deal with his patients. Joyous as he was, he knew he could never call her up and propose something so childish.

Their relationship was more complicated than that.

Nathan returned to his barstool, theatrically adjusting his glasses. "'Twas the Raven, my man."

"I'm glad one of us knows Poe."

He checked his text messages and Will clucked his tongue in passing as he turned in his team's answer.

"No phones, professor."

"You come talk to me in about 10 years when you have a pregnant wife to deal with, Will Morris."

"That kid is irritating." Dayton welcomed the gummy eyeball into his mouth, cheeks puckering at the sour melon flavor. "It's no wonder his parents got a divorce."

"You know what, Dayton? Every day I thank our lord and savior that you're not a child psychiatrist." He held up a finger to Sasha, signaling for another beer.

They both burst into laughter, which was such a rare event that Nathan seemed genuinely startled but their hysterics soon fizzled out. The Halloween music looped. Michael, the host, had stepped away to use the bathroom and songs that were tolerable sandwiched between trivia questions became unbearable. Dayton was primed for an aneurysm when the opening notes of 'Monster Mash' played.

Mercifully, Michael soon returned, grabbing the mic with the nonchalance of someone who hadn't interrupted a public game night with a 10-minute restroom break.

"Alright, folks, we're going to switch gears a little bit with a few TV and movie questions. I want you to tell me who played Jason Vor—"

The rear entry door slammed against the wall and a hush fell over the room. A line cook stood in the open doorway. He had plugs the size of saucers and his eyes were stretched just as wide.

"Sasha, call the B.S.P.D. and tell 'em to come over here pronto. There's a chick in the dumpster and she ain't drunk if you know what I mean."

Sasha's frantic movements were rendered comical with faux spiderwebs woven into her hair as she battled the clunky landline, delivering the news in a shaking voice as her hand cupped the receiver. Dayton drained the rest of his drink before the cops stormed the place.

At first, it was only a pair of officers. Then a second car came, and a third. They were in and out of the rear door, mumbling into the radios perched on their shoulders and to each other.

"Secure the premises."

"Nobody leaves this bar until we get statements from everyone. So get comfortable."

The two original officers who had arrived on the scene split the duty of collecting statements. Others rolled out yellow tape, placed placards on the ground out back, and flashed pictures. Some of the patrons' faces had grown pale and clammy. The Halloween theme had gotten too real.

Soon, the coroner turned up.

A few girls gasped as they caught the briefest glimpse of a ghastly, pale blue body being delicately exhumed from the dumpster. Someone released a blood-curdling scream. Another fell to the floor.

"Oh, hell no." Sasha knelt behind the bar and the crass sound of her vomiting made others recoil.

"Good lord," Nathan muttered.

Dayton succeeded in looking on without affect but the breath he held revealed his true feelings.

With startling efficiency, a black body bag was stuffed, zipped, and rolled around to the front of the bar where it was loaded into a white truck.

"I hope my pregnant wife is alright. At home. Alone." Nathan raised his voice enough so that the nearest officers would hear. They didn't acknowledge him in the slightest.

All around them, organized panic played out.

He hadn't realized the music had stopped until another round of wailing police cars cut their engines. More cops. Their uniforms revealed that they weren't local. Portland.

How long had it been since they were forbidden from leaving the bar? There was no traffic at that time of night. Even with clear roads, it took at least 45 minutes to get from Portland to Branch Spring.

It had gone from two officers collecting statements to six, not including the one dedicated to grilling the line cook. Occasionally, they broke away from the routine questioning to pass along updates. The disgruntled comments had less to do with useful insight regarding the crime scene and more to do with the fact that some guy named Reynolds wouldn't be able to make it out until the following morning.

Dayton complied with the officers along with everyone else and after another hour they were released. He left calmly, getting into his car and pulling onto the road as if he hadn't just had a brush with the entirety of the greater Portland area's law enforcement.

With a sputtering heart and a questionable blood-alcohol level, he sped off into the bleak October night.

15

LACEY

Dayton

*H*e and Kenna sat side by side on the sofa in the living room of her apartment—somewhere he never thought he'd be permitted entrance again and yet there he was.

Though the foot of space separating them on the sofa was a reminder that they were still recovering from her discovery of his misdeeds.

Dayton continued to curse himself for the folly. He should've burned that box long before she ever set foot in his home. Even after knowing Kenna for only a few blissful weeks, he knew everything was meant to end with her, as if her appearance in his life had been divinely orchestrated by the universe. But now that destiny was barely hanging on.

Threadbare.

Every time he found himself frustrated with their stationary position on the timeline of their would-be relationship, he was faced with the painful realization that he was to blame for their lack of motion.

He wasn't entirely sure why she had invited him over that evening, but he knew better than to complain when each second spent with her felt like a gift.

Ephemeral bursts of joy of which he simultaneously felt unworthy and greedily accepted.

She hadn't spoken more than two words to him since his arrival and the uncharacteristic behavior triggered a wave of panic within him, undulating throughout his body and heightening his senses one by one.

Maybe Kenna had asked him here to terminate their relationship that had never truly begun. A premature death.

He would mourn the loss but, ultimately, he'd have to accept it. Tempting as it was, Dayton could not hold her prisoner. She had been his salvation, and if that was the lone purpose for their having met, so be it, for he now knew how to love and he'd carry that with him forever. And when he perished, a part of him would glow eternally because embedded within him was something that evaded so many others.

Love, that glorious blinding light.

"Shouldn't you be out with your friends?" It was a question better left unasked and yet he dared to ask it.

Her presence at the apartment supported the idea that she'd invited him over for company. She was studious. Lonely. Much like he had been in medical school and later still during residency.

"Things are pretty bleak in the friendship department these days."

"What about those kids on your trivia team?"

His question inadvertently triggered flashbacks to the previous night. Police lights. Yellow tape. Anxious faces.

"We aren't on speaking terms. You should know that. You were there."

At 22, she was already a seasoned wife despite her unwed status. There was no getting anything past her.

The clicking and churning of metal sounded at the front door and Dayton supposed the mechanical melodies belonged to none other than the new roommate. He knew Alex had returned to Phoenix but knew nothing of the young woman who now paid the other half of the rent.

She entered the apartment, all flowing hair and a whirl of jasmine perfume so intense, he smelled it from the sofa.

"I just dropped by to ch—" her speech halted as she spun to face them. A tiny golden flower adorned her right nostril. Her taupe lips bloomed into a smile. "Sorry to barge in like this. I didn't know you had a guest."

The thinly veiled panic on Kenna's face said it all. This was an introduction she did not wish to make.

Quiet bravery prevailed. "This is Liza, my roommate."

He waited a beat for her to introduce him but she did no such thing and Liza's polite smile became too much to bear amid the distilled silence.

"So you're the new roommate." Rising, he crossed the room and offered his hand to her, which she shook without reservation. "I'm Dayton. Kenna's boyfriend."

"Hello boyfriend who I've heard absolutely nothing about." Her brown eyes cut to Kenna before they settled back on him. "I just stopped by to change my shoes. I'll be out all night so you two lovebirds won't have to worry about me."

He swore he felt Kenna's muted fury radiating to where he stood by the island. No matter how much his version of an intro-duction had upset her, he was certain that, had he identified himself as 'Dr. Merino,' he would've been ousted from the apart-ment right behind Liza. Defying all expectations, she did not yell at him when he rejoined her.

She breathed a soft "thank you."

Moments later, Liza emerged from the hallway and scarcely offered a mumbled goodbye as she barreled out the door. Dayton grabbed the remote and flipped through the channels. During the shuffle, a hair-raising broadcast played for half a second before it was replaced by another station.

His silent prayer that Kenna had not noticed the horror temporarily plastered on the screen went unanswered.

"Go back."

He obeyed and fought to keep his cortisol level from spiking as she watched the coverage, engrossed. Sweat beaded along his spine. In his mind, he had done no wrong and yet his body insisted upon his guilt.

Kenna

Everything within her froze as the blue and red lights flashed behind the reporter on the screen and she parsed out the only words that mattered among the graphics.

Body found.

The bold, ugly phrase. So much despair crammed into its brevity.

She imagined the sorority sisters were watching it too. Kenna felt their collective flash of denial before it pirouetted into rage. She heard their mangled screams and choked sobs as they yelled at the television and yanked on their coats, not bothering to turn it off as they filed through the door en route to storming the crime scene.

It was all too easy to imagine how they must have felt. The thought alone of losing one of her sisters shattered her iced over insides.

She turned the volume up.

"The body found Thursday evening discarded in a downtown dumpster has been identified as Lacey Greene, a 21-year-old undergrad at Ponderosa University who was reported missing late last week. Greene's body was discovered by an employee of The Rusted Monkey while taking out the garbage."

Slowly, her head turned to Dayton as a wall of tears rose behind her eyes. She was hollow and capable of nothing else but the silent, accusatory look.

"You think I did this?"

His question was a whisper loaded with words he was afraid to vocalize.

Is it what she thought? Sorting her feelings on the issue seemed to be the least sensible course of action with a potential murderer in her apartment.

"You could've helped her, Dayton. You had the means and you sat idly by. And you may not have been the one to kill her, but Lacey's death is on your hands."

He pushed to his feet, animosity clouding his expression. "Do you know why I didn't help her? *You.* You were fucking with my head, my heart, my everything. I wasn't passing clear judgment."

"Don't blame it on me. That's ridiculous." Kenna's voice had gone so quiet, she hardly recognized it as her own.

Strands of fear and unease crocheted her organs until all she felt was a unified sense of foreboding. Again, she remembered his soul-splitting gaze in St. James on Christmas Eve. The warning from God she had ignored.

"You know what the sad part is? It wouldn't surprise me that much if you were the one who did this."

Dayton paced the length of the coffee table and clasped his hands behind his neck for a second before they burst into movement. "You've always been quick to accuse me, but what about you? You're not innocent here."

"I'm not a killer."

"No? You're a liar. That's a start, isn't it?"

"I don't know what you're talking about."

Truly, Kenna didn't. Her head teemed with tears and possibilities as the grim broadcast droned on with the aim of making its audience feel something by spouting off things like 'sorority member' and 'honor student.'

His face was neutral but there was something frightening about it. She spotted the Caprice keys on the island and thought about lunging for them. Trying her luck.

But she knew how quick Dayton was.

"Sure you do. You may not have sent that email to O.M.B., but I know you went to the police."

He stared at her with a forbidding stillness and no one was around to witness her demise. She had no intention of being the next girl found in a dumpster.

It felt as if Kenna had swallowed an anchor, its flukes puncturing either side of her throat. "Dayton, I—"

"Hush, lamb."

Silence engulfed the room as he turned off the television. He crossed his arms, looking more betrayed than anything else.

"I'd found happiness. I'd found it with you, and when you finally came to your senses and returned, I didn't care that you were bearing threats. I knew they were empty, that you wouldn't dare do anything with your so-called evidence and that, even if you did, I wouldn't face any legal consequences. But I didn't expect you to go through with it, and when I found out that you had ..." He shut his eyes, drawing in a deep breath. "Well, I was beside myself."

The Dayton she knew had gone. She was listening to someone else speak. Patrick Bateman. Neither man allowed morals to form a barrier between them and what they wanted.

"The police were highly dismissive of me."

"The fact remains, you went. You want to see me punished in some way. Tell me, what crime have I committed?"

The challenge had her on her feet in an instant. She stood toe to toe with the devil. No longer afraid of death.

"Have you considered that, maybe, my going to the police wasn't about you?" She shouted in his face and it was such a rush, something she'd wanted to do for a long time. "I've been trying to figure you out since we met. Knowing everything that I do about you is an incredible burden and not being able to discuss it with anyone is an even greater one. I thought the police would at least listen. Maybe a small part of me hoped it led to something more, a search warrant, *something* to make you realize that the way you behave is wrong."

Dayton didn't shout or ring her neck or attempt to defend himself in any way against her slew of what bordered on verbal assault. He was rigid, emotionless.

"Stop looking at your keys and leave. That's what you do when things become too much, isn't it? Run away. It's what you did after we slept together. You ran away from me like you ran away from your family."

"You don't know anything about my family."

"No. Only what you've told me, but it's enough. Or have you forgotten that I help people process trauma for a living?" He stepped closer. "Do you think you're uniquely difficult to figure out? You aren't."

Kenna barreled past him and swiped the car keys off the island and was out the door, not realizing until she was halfway down the stairs that she'd left her own apartment instead of kicking him out.

Her flight response was in full force.

Soon, she was behind the wheel of the Caprice, heading for the one place that would welcome her at any hour.

Faint, flickering light set the stained glass of St. James aglow as Kenna climbed the steps. Inside, her footsteps echoed against the stone and they summoned a voice from somewhere in the recesses of the nave.

"Do you wish to seek confession?"

She swallowed but it only exacerbated the lump in her throat. "Yes, Father."

"Come along."

The priest disappeared into one side of the booth and she

entered the other, kneeling on the step. Her breaths sounded harsh and heavy in the confined space. Her pulse hadn't settled from the scene at the apartment. The priest was silent as he waited for her to begin.

Lacey was dead, and for some inexplicable reason, she felt responsible in part for her death.

Though they'd met only once, she had been the epitome of a cry for help. The bruised neck and swollen eyes. But Dayton had shut down her insistence that he intervene. A pang lacerated her chest and she wondered if there was a reason he had denied her help.

In a darker corner of her mind, she wondered if he had been the boyfriend whom Lacey had spoken of. Kenna was no stranger to his love and bruises and the addictive properties they carried.

"Bless me Father, for I have sinned. My last confession was five months ago."

She had started attending Mass again after the falling-out with Dayton, when she'd woken up from the spell he had placed her under only to realize she had strayed from God.

"Someone needed my help, and I did nothing. Maybe, if I'd said something, I could've saved them."

"Child, we cannot go back, only forward. What matters is that you are here, in this moment, seeking penance. If this person you speak of has perished, take comfort in the knowledge that it was God's will."

Kenna bit her tongue lest she demanded the priest explain to her how a murder was the will of God.

The advice was limited and tired, but she supposed if she had to sit inside a booth every day and absorb the confessions of the guilty she'd too run out of useful things to say. She thanked him and they each prayed before she slipped out of St. James into the veil of night. A raindrop plopped on the crown of her head, followed by another, as she pulled her coat tighter to guard against the wind.

She imagined it was Lacey's way of letting her know she was at peace. No longer suffering.

A tightness ruled Kenna's throat once inside the station wagon, wondering if her tears would one day soon fall from the sky. If it was God's will to rip her from the fabric of creation.

November

16

WHERE WE LEFT THINGS

Kenna

*A*n enlarged print of Dayton's Polaroid collection rested on the cold metal table between Kenna and a pair of cops. They had listened to her frantic rambling with passive faces. Now they seemed ready to throw her out onto the street without sparing an iota of consideration.

The thinner of the two officers pushed the print toward her. "I'm sorry, ma'am, but there isn't anything we can do with this."

She clutched it to her chest and stared at them, as if her penetrative gaze would somehow bestow them with an ounce of empathy. "You're absolutely sure?"

"They're just pictures. There's no signs of foul play within them and we'd need at least that to even stir consideration for a search warrant, at which point we'd hope to find those images, but they'd likely be gone. But the pictures you've shown us don't indicate anything malicious. Perverted, sure."

"So, that's it?"

"Yes, ma'am."

She headed for the door, but as her hand clutched the knob, the larger officer called to her.

"Oh, and hun? The next time you come down here and try to slander an upstanding member of our community, try bringing some real evidence."

Kenna pushed herself up on her palms. Cold sweat soaked her temples. Her shut laptop lay amid the comforter.

Once her pulse leveled out and rational thought returned, she supposed falling asleep while reviewing the Polaroids had acted as an open invitation for the unpleasant dream. The officers, though infuriating, had been right.

No signs of foul play.

The one remotely abusive thing she would've been able to prove was the bite-induced bruise spanning her shoulder, but her body was contorted in a way that obscured it. She wondered if Dayton had intentionally shifted her before taking the shot. Her finger wiggled on the trackpad, and the image reappeared on the screen. Everyone else was on their back, no suspicious arrangement of sheets or posture.

Maybe he had turned Kenna to fit the narrative of the way he saw them together. He didn't want to remember her as another person he'd hurt.

Saint Kenna. She studied her sleeping form, the white lingerie and moonlight, and wondered whether that was who she'd truly become. A sinner's saint.

Frustration welled in her throat as she stared at the inscriptions in black ink. The absence of last names rendered them one half of an unsolvable puzzle and, in that moment of quiet defeat, she realized how futile the hunt for answers had become. Yet a low-burning flame within her insisted that she keep going.

Lacey, with her purple skin and plaid scarf.

While she wasn't sure if Dayton had hurt her—let alone been

the one responsible for her death—she'd be damned if she didn't find out.

She jumped as a shrill ding came from her phone and she strained to reach it on the nightstand. Her stomach twisted upon seeing whose name was spelled out across the notification banner.

> D: I don't love where we left things. Would you be willing to meet at Bigleaf? Nice and public.

Kenna resented how he had tacked on the bit at the end, as if she genuinely feared he'd hack her to pieces.

Chewing the inside of her cheek, she reread the message several times. She knew she had hit a wall with the dirt she had collected on him and reasoned it may have been unlikely that she'd uncover anything further unless she assured him she was on his side.

Play the part of the lover.

She responded to his text and rolled out of bed, rushing around her room and pulling clothes on as her fingers attempted to tame her bed head into a semi-smooth plait.

Liza was stationed at the kitchen island when she emerged. She peeled and stuck flags, on which she wrote careful annotations, in her textbook. Her usual black cold brew set off to the side, sweating all over the counter.

"You look nice for someone who just woke up. Big date this early?"

Kenna swiped her purse off the vacant stool and didn't bother forcing a smile. "Something like that."

She hated lying to Liza. Perhaps it wasn't technically lying, but she felt it was dishonest to withhold Dayton's true identity. Kenna had assured her the rumors weren't true and she had unwittingly met the man at the center of them.

Chin resting in her palm, Liza narrowed her eyes mischievously. "I can't believe you hid an entire boyfriend from me. He's pretty handsome, too. Maybe not in the cliché way where women fall to their knees when he walks by, but he's mysterious and broody and that's kind of hot. Can I be honest, though? He's a bit old."

She had a point. It wasn't something Kenna had ever considered—their ages. They matched wits well enough despite their differing levels of education and while they were far from equals, they could carry on a conversation without losing interest or becoming confused by one another.

What else mattered?

"Can't fault you there. I'll be back later," she said, one foot already out the door, wincing as Liza called after her.

"Love Island?"

"Must we?"

"The gods demand it, Ace."

Dayton

His stomach had been tense since his morning run.

The scene at Kenna's apartment had unraveled faster than he could comprehend. Dayton swiftly lost his composure over her accusations. He had kept his cool at the bar that fateful night, but it was more demanding to keep a level head when the person spewing venom was the one you held the most dear. He had already lost her once.

He refused to let her slip through his fingers again.

Almost every table in Bigleaf was taken when he arrived. To make matters worse, they were jammed close together. He ordered their coffees and planted the placard on the table in the middle of the shop as if he were claiming a territory. Some of the patrons dragged their eyes from their laptops to give him dirty looks but he took a seat and ignored them, watching the door.

The barista delivered their order and he hardly produced a rushed 'thank you' as Kenna came through the front door and joined him at the table. She was barefaced and sloppily dressed, the latter of which was uncharacteristic, but even so her presence across from him had his heart stuttering.

"We both said some regretful things the other night."

Her gaze swept the room before settling on him, and though it was filled with ire it disbanded the lingering tension in his abdomen. "You didn't come in here and immediately think that us being seen together might be a bad idea?"

"We have no control over how people perceive us, only in the way we carry ourselves."

She leaned into the table, bringing their faces marginally closer, her voice a dangerous whisper. "And how do you suppose I carry myself when other people think of me as a slut? Someone who's, quote, fucking her way through college."

"You and I both know the truth."

"I don't know if I can freely associate you with the truth." Kenna took a ginger sip of her latte. "There had better be a good reason you dragged me out of bed this early on the weekend. Other than humiliating me in a café full of people, of course."

"I want to discuss Lacey."

Her fingers stilled on the mug.

"Do you?"

"Yes. I can't begin to fathom why you'd accuse me of such a thing. I haven't been able to sleep knowing that's how you see me."

She hurled his words back at him, laced with malice. "You should learn to carry yourself better."

Dayton's throat constricted. Clever girl.

His nails dug into the underside of the table as he fought to maintain a modicum of composure.

"I love you, Kenna Aisling, and it feels like a betrayal of the highest degree that you think I'm the one responsible for this."

"That day in your office, you wouldn't help her. She had bruises all over her neck and you did nothing and weeks later, you were giving me bruises."

"Do you hear yourself? You sound like a conspiracy theorist. That isn't a logical line of thinking."

"Maybe you'd consider my other point of contention to be more logical." Folding her arms on the table, she leaned across them, speaking only where he could hear. "Sometimes I wonder, what if Bella didn't jump?"

Kenna was right. The choice of venue had been a poor idea. It was imperative he stayed calm despite his boiling blood, that quiet inferno. He inhaled sharply to steady himself.

"Stand up and walk outside. Forget the coffee."

Eyes widening, she obeyed in mute terror and Dayton trailed behind her out the door. He grabbed her hand to ensure she remained at his side.

She always seemed to be running.

Brilliant red leaves fell from the youthful maples and floated to the ground. Piles collected in the gutter. They strolled along the sidewalk of Branch Spring's historic downtown, hand in hand, and the other couples passing by were none the wiser that he was holding her hostage to their conversation.

"Bella was sick long before she and I met. Her decision to take her life had nothing to do with our involvement. Did we not settle this fear of yours at Sinclair's?"

She tried to jerk her hand free but he tightened his grasp. "You expect me to chalk it up to coincidence that she died three days after you slept with her? I mean, really, if she was as sick as you say, why did you sacrifice her treatment over getting her in bed?"

So much for the walk.

Dayton pulled her into an alleyway and pinned her shoulders to the brick, craning his neck and staring wildly into her eyes. "I didn't end Bella's treatment. She did. When she mentioned ending her sessions, she asked me if I'd walk with her in the park one evening. She said fresh air did more for her than sitting in a shrink's office. So I thought I'd be progressive and agree. She kissed me on those trails and I knew I was playing with fire, choosing her, but my lust can't be swayed once it's made up its mind."

"Like Lacey?"

He drove her shoulders further into the wall. "No, not like Lacey. I couldn't have had her even if I'd wanted to. I'd already chosen you."

She was far from moved by the sentiment.

"If you haven't hurt anyone, why do you insist on filling my head with these dark fantasies? What you said at your house about *organs* in jars? The mind games have to stop."

Dayton knew he had taken their conversation on the couch too far but his fear of the way she viewed him had taken charge and ran with it.

Yet another thing out of his control.

Dropping his forehead to hers, he ignored the way she flinched. Her recoil tugged at something deep within his chest. It uprooted his heart. He had tried to convince Kenna that he was a monster in small part because he didn't believe he deserved her. That didn't mean he wanted her any less.

She was a ray of light in his eternal night.

"It's telling how little experience you have in this world, going around and believing such an outlandish remark."

"Who made you an authority on my experience?"

"The comment about why your parents wouldn't let any of you learn to drive? It doesn't take much more than that to figure out that you were sheltered, though I don't know to what extent. Maybe one day, I will." Dayton channeled a new energy in his gaze. More sincere, less intense. He laced his fingers with hers and she drew a sharp intake of breath, like she had regressed to an age where hand-holding was scandalous. "But until then, I'll thank God every day, knowing He could have brought you anywhere and yet He chose to lead you here."

It was the truth. It was all he had, the antidote for whatever pain he'd inflicted on her.

He only hoped it was enough.

17

BODY LANGUAGE

Dayton

*H*e hardly felt better about where he stood with Kenna after their disastrous chat in the alleyways downtown. Staying in contact with her was enough; he wouldn't be greedy. Besides, he was thoroughly convinced he could not make her see reason.

It was up to her to determine his guilt or innocence.

All morning, Dayton was stationed at his desk. His research had ended with Kenna but he'd been neglectful of compiling his findings. He copied and pasted and burned holes into the keyboard as he typed, all the while wondering if he'd be finishing the near decade-long project in vain.

With Kenna, he had stumbled into an unexpected outcome. It was best to quit while he was ahead. Forget the project and turn to what he wanted most: happiness.

The doorbell rang. His fingers hovered over the keys.

As he approached the door, he was light with anticipation in the hope that Kenna was on the other side.

Perhaps she wanted to apologize for how out of hand things had gotten after they'd breezed out of Bigleaf. She'd collapse into his arms, an incoherent flurry of 'I'm sorry's. He'd hold her while she admitted how remorseful she was to have accused him of such treachery.

Dayton opened the door, revealing a man with a pointed face in a suit and dark sunglasses. His hair was a dirty shade of blonde that bordered on brunette. Short but somehow unkempt. He glanced behind the man, spotting a black, nondescript SUV parked along the street, and his skin prickled as wariness set in.

The stranger smiled. All lips, no teeth.

"Glad I caught you at home. You weren't around yesterday when I stopped by." He whipped out a badge from within the breast of his jacket. "I'm Detective Brian Reynolds with the Portland Police Bureau. I'm the lead on the Greene investigation."

Reynolds.

The man the other officers had spoken of at the bar.

The detective stepped past him, operating under the assumption that a flash of his badge negated formal permission to enter. An aroma of stale cigarettes and cheap car air freshener followed him inside.

"Please, have a seat." It was the last thing he wanted to say, but he lacked any alternative.

How would it look if he didn't cooperate with an investigation? He wasn't surprised it had come to this.

The poor girl hadn't put herself in that dumpster.

Reynolds took the armchair while, after much internal debate, he sat in the middle of the couch. The rightmost side would've made him seem too evasive. Had he chosen the leftmost side, he would've seemed too eager.

The detective retrieved an impossibly small notebook from the outer pocket of his jacket. The leather harness holster cutting across his dress shirt didn't escape Dayton's notice.

"Let me check my notes. I get a little mixed up sometimes."

Atop the cushion, his hands tightened into fists before loosening again as he watched the detective flip through those tiny pages.

"I've been hopping around town the last few days, following up on a couple of things from the statements my guys pulled."

Dayton didn't care for the explanation but it miffed him nonetheless. He couldn't think of a single incriminating thing that resided in the statement he'd given.

"You *are* Dayton Merino, correct? That's the name I have for this address."

"Yes."

"Dayton Merino." He said again, this time in a questioning tone. "Feel like I know that name. You're a doctor, is that right?" He was quiet for a beat. A wedding band glinted in the natural light as he flipped another page. "Psychiatry?"

"That's right."

If the rest of the questioning went on like this, Dayton was sure he'd lose whatever shred of sanity he still had. Asking questions to which the detective already knew the answers.

Be cordial, responsive, he silently coached.

"You worked at the university up until recently?"

"Yes. I left after the spring term."

"Why?"

"Is that relevant?"

Reynolds shrugged. "Could be."

"I resigned. There were … rumors, about myself and a student whom I mentored."

"Rumors," he repeated.

"Of the career-halting variety."

"I see what you're getting at." He scribbled a note. "So, you have a practice over in East Haven? I rode by there earlier today. Nice place."

Dayton didn't like where this was heading. Just how hard was the detective looking into him?

"Yes."

"And have you continued to treat any of your patients from the university at the new practice?"

"A few."

"Was Lacey Greene among them?"

"She was not." He answered honestly, though it was clear from Reynolds' dismissive nod that it didn't matter. He had something.

"I find that pretty interesting." He sank further into the chair, elbows hooked over its arms, and it was evident he'd been in that very position innumerable times. "You see, doc, we've been reviewing traffic camera footage in Branch Spring and the surrounding towns in the days following Lacey's disappearance, and we came across something a little odd. Friday, October 23rd, 11:33 a.m., we've got her standing outside your practice talking to you. Even more curious, judging by the body language, it seems like the two of you had some sort of disagreement. And, to clarify, by 'seems like' I mean clear as fucking day." Something cold and unforgiving flickered across his face. "So, you understand why I might have a few questions about that. Especially considering you also *happened* to be at the bar the night her body was found."

Scenes of Lacey overwhelmed him. The mascara tracks on her cheeks and her choked sobs. Her raw wrists and bare feet. Kenna's voice rang out in his head like a church bell, loud and inescapable. *You could've helped her, Dayton.*

"I attend trivia night every Thursday at the bar. Religiously. As for Lacey ... she sought me out for help. I couldn't give it."

"Do you remember any of that exchange?"

"I was trying to talk her down, but she was hysterical, saying the same thing over and over. Eventually, I raised my voice in an effort to get through to her." Despite the quiver in his stomach, he offered a pertinent detail. Playing to Reynolds seemed to be the obvious route. "Her wrists were red, like she'd been tied up."

"Rope burn." He nodded. "We already checked out the boyfriend's house. Photographed the whole twisted setup. The fucker had her locked away in the basement. Now, if I had things my way, I'd hold him down at the precinct and make him sweat 'til he was singing like a canary. Bad news is, he skipped town. So, I was hoping you might be able to give me a little intel about her and this boyfriend. Shane Sanders."

"Psychotherapist-patient privilege, I'm afraid."

"You and I both know that ethical mumbo jumbo doesn't extend beyond the grave."

"Well, detective, whenever this case goes to trial, if you were to argue that Lacey's death was a result of her psychiatric state, then I'd have no choice but to release those details. However, Lacey didn't suffer from any definable condition. She only needed someone to lend an ear."

"Where were you on the evening of October 23rd?"

"Owens-Adair. On Fridays, I work the night shift in the emergency department. Psych intakes and evals."

He stared at Dayton as if he were trying to shake him down but the look soon bloomed into one of recognition.

"I remember you. That girl who jumped off the roof at the university. What was her name? Mc-something."

"Bella McAnders. Yes, that was … unfortunate."

"We spoke over the phone."

"Can't say I recall. She's not the first patient I've lost."

"Huh. I was still at Branch Spring's P.D. back then." Reynolds gestured between them. "This is about as full circle as you can get. Years later, sitting here, talking to you about a different case."

After a couple more questions that were far less intimidating, he tucked his notebook inside his jacket pocket and rose from the armchair.

Dayton didn't remember saying goodbye but he must have as Reynolds saluted him like an overgrown boy scout as he ducked out the front door.

Left alone with a thundering heart and ringing ears.

18
TRUST

Dayton

*D*ayton clutched a bouquet of garnet roses, the same ones he'd given Kenna on her birthday. The bitter, cold wind rose and fell like a silent Gershwin symphony. He crossed the street half a block shy of the crosswalk.

Caution abandoned those who were in love.

Still, he wasn't entirely without caution. He fought the urge to stare at the post on his way across the street. Glaring at the traffic camera that caught his exchange with Lacey would've been ill-advised.

It was something as simple as noticing the camera that sent the brief but panic-inspiring interaction with Detective Reynolds to the forefront of his mind. The questions and the extended pauses and the silent accusations buried within his looks. Weeks had passed and the meeting continued to haunt him.

Hand curled around the bar on the practice door, he banished those thoughts. He needed a distraction. A chance to get away from the investigation that was slowly bleeding into his life; and, unbeknownst to Kenna, she was going to accompany him.

The digital chimes went off as he pushed the door open and she fleetingly glanced up from whatever coursework she was undoubtedly working on. He'd always found her beautiful in that deep state of concentration.

He laid the flowers on the corner of the reception desk. "I want to speak with you before you leave this afternoon. Say okay."

"Okay."

"Tell the patient I'm ready."

Dayton toed off toward the session space. A light perspiration clung to his skin, a byproduct of the anticipation of the conversation they'd have later.

Kenna's sweet voice rang out in the waiting area.

"Dr. Merino will see you now, Ms. Griffith."

It was so very different from the tone she used with him. The inherent kindness in her voice dried up. He liked to think it was her real voice, but no one else had ever coaxed it out of her.

He dutifully spent his 60 minutes with Ms. Griffith and was quite pleased with the level of attentiveness he'd managed to spare her despite the subtle trace of anxiety gently rippling through his chest.

Tiny white caps on a calm day at sea.

After the patient had gone, he awaited Kenna's presence in his private office. The approaching clack of Mary Janes on the tile soon gave way to her hovering by the doorjamb.

"You brought flowers and summoned me to your office. This doesn't sound good."

He rose and met her in the doorway, guiding her by the small of her back to the desk chair. Dayton lightly pushed her thighs until she took a hint and sat down.

"You're making me nervous," she said.

He seized her hands, relishing in their heat as it spread across his icy palms. Kenna looked at him, and though it was marred with worry, he recognized the affection she had for him shining like diamonds amid those emerald pools. She'd never said it aloud but that moment transcended language.

"I want you to meet my family."

She hung her head, peeking at him through her eyelashes. "Dayton, that doesn't make sense. I'm a grad student who you slept with once. Not to mention the troubling detail that I work for you 20 hours a week."

"So we have to smooth over a few details."

"You're going to lie to your parents?"

"Not lie. Omit." His hand sailed through his hair. "My sister always visits them for Thanksgiving and she tries to rope me into it every year without much luck, but this time when she called, I told her I'd be there and that I was bringing someone special."

It was the truth, despite her inevitable suspicion. He'd told Carmen he would bring Kenna along for the holiday. Of course, he hadn't realized then that the trip would serve as a convenient way to rid himself of the infuriating detective.

For a few days, anyway.

He studied her face as her expression morphed from disbelief to annoyance to confusion and back again.

"Basically, you sat me down to tell me that I'm going with you, rather than asking me like a rational human being, because they're already operating under the assumption that *we* are coming?"

Staring at her blankly, he said, "Yes."

"Why is it so important to you that I meet them? It's not as if we're in a ..." Her hesitation hurt and he was relieved she did not finish the thought.

"We've spent a great deal of time together, have we not? And I've made you aware of my feelings. Now, I'm under the impression that you and I cannot move forward in any meaningful way until some of this," he performed a circular gesture, "hatred you have for me dissolves."

And I'd like to evade the authorities on the off chance that they come

119

after me in the boyfriend's absence. Reynolds had a bloodthirsty look in his eyes.

The details really aren't important, darling.

"I don't hate you, it's just—"

"Maybe not. At the very least, you're wary of me. It's like a toxicant in the air, polluting our potential. Come with me. Meet my family. I pray it'll give you a new perspective."

She gazed out the metal blind imprisoned window. It was perhaps the longest moment of Dayton's life. On his knees, at her mercy.

"When do we leave?"

Kenna

She wasn't sure what had possessed her to surrender to Dayton's ridiculous request but there was no denying the reality as she packed her bag the following week.

She had said yes.

It took everything within Kenna to keep her dark and dreadful thoughts at bay. Paranoia-drenched fears that were better off forgotten. But paranoia was a persistent beast, one which gnawed on its victim's every nerve ending until they succumbed to whatever visions it had conjured.

Her nerves were raw. She accepted the visions. Her fears took the stage and she was the lone audience member.

Gripping a sweater in her hands, her mind whisked her away from her bedroom and into Dayton's sports car. He drove fast, so fast that the familiar scenery of the tree lined road was difficult to distinguish through the passenger window. Even at breakneck speed, she knew they hadn't left Branch Spring. Had they been heading for Eugene, they would've been on the interstate.

Miles and miles ago.

The car slowed, engine purring, as he pulled over into a bank of grass. Her heart hammered in her chest as he stared out the windshield before languidly fixing his gaze on her.

"I'm sorry it had to be this way, lamb."

Kenna shut her eyes with such force, they stung, but the discomfort didn't phase her as the horrific fantasy disbanded. It was something she'd feared at the beginning of the year that had carried little weight until Dayton had crushed his hand to her throat. His killing her.

As she filled her duffel bag, she grew more and more convinced that the trip was a thinly veiled cover to get her alone. She had too much damning information on him and she'd tried to make use out of some of it during her fruitless visit to the police station. And though Kenna had not yet nailed the scope of it, he was dangerous.

She understood that, when she climbed into his car the next morning, willing and alive, there was no guarantee she'd exit in the same condition.

Bile scaled her throat. She thought of her sisters.

So much time had passed since she'd heard any of their voices over the phone but she could easily imagine the sound of their broken cries over the news of her death.

How long before the news reached them in a house without television, with computers mandated as use for homework only, and radio stations too zeroed in on intrastate dealings to be concerned with whatever was going on in the rest of the country?

"Liza," Kenna called.

She didn't want to involve her, truly. But the possibility that her sisters may not hear anything for weeks in the event of her untimely death was one she could not stomach.

Liza glanced between her and the duffel bag. "Need help packing for your romantic getaway?"

"No," she said softly. Kenna sat on the bed and gestured to the empty space before her. "Will you sit, please? I need to talk to you."

She complied. "Should I be worried?"

"That's up to you, I suppose."

Liza quirked a brow.

For a beat, Kenna wondered whether dragging Liza into things was a good idea. They weren't nearly as close as she and Alex had been. Then of course, they hadn't told each other everything, either.

"Can I trust you?"

"Of course."

"Look, I haven't been honest with you."

"How so?"

"The day in the bookstore when you asked me if the rumors were true, I lied. And no, not everything they're saying is true, but I did sleep with him."

"Ace."

It was a quiet disappointment. No anger.

"There's more." Kenna tucked her knees to her chest. "He's who I've been working for in East Haven. He has a private practice there." She siphoned a deep breath that burned her lungs. "The guy who was over before? That was him. Dr. Merino."

"Well, it's not so hard to see why you slept with him, then. Mysterious and broody, remember?"

Tears welling, she shook her head. "There's another side to him, Liza, and I decided to tell you all of this because I'm leaving in the morning and … there's a chance I won't come back. I wanted someone to know who I left with."

Now Liza was the one shaking her head.

"If you're in that much trouble," her eyes went wild, "if you think he's going to *hurt* you? It would be stupid to go."

"It's not a question of if." Kenna spoke through gritted teeth, fearing that there was no other way to rid herself of the damned words. "I'm going."

She had to understand him, his behavior.

Even if it killed her.

19

EUGENE

Dayton

*D*ayton breathed a sigh of relief when Wednesday morning rolled around and he stood on the mat outside Kenna's apartment. Reynolds had not sought him out for further follow-up questions. No phone call or impromptu visit. It made him hopeful that he and Kenna could, eventually, move on from this.

Sure, it would take some time for her to get over—what she referred to as negligence on his part—the loss of Lacey when they had a small window to intervene.

But Kenna hadn't pulled back enough to see all of the details. That window was in disrepair. Smudged fingerprints on the interior. The girl tried to let herself out, for how long? There were splinters in the glass, shards missing in some places from the many people who'd wanted to help her escape. She had been a prisoner to that cycle: wanting to free herself, the doubt that ensued, seeking help from others but then realizing it was only the concept of being rescued that she liked.

Kenna may not have recognized it, but he did.

The silent tug-of-war in Lacey's eyes before she stormed out of his university office.

He rapped once on the door and footsteps approached from within. It was soon opened by her roommate.

"Hello, boyfriend." Liza smiled but it didn't come as easily as the one she'd displayed during their first meeting.

There was something guarded about her friendliness. Or perhaps that was her resting expression in which case there was nothing unusual about it. Dayton wondered if he was overdue for his own psychiatric evaluation.

A tic came over his jaw as he registered the shower running in the background.

"Would you let her know I'm downstairs?"

"Sure thing."

He retreated down the steps and waited in the car, contemplating whether she was having second thoughts or if she simply had no regard for punctuality. No, that wasn't it. More often than not, she was early rather than late.

Twenty minutes later, Kenna crouched and peered at him through the passenger side window, pulling the handle to no avail as her speech echoed through the glass.

"Let me in."

With a flick of his index finger, he unlocked the car and she collapsed in the passenger seat, bag in her lap. He promptly grabbed it and discarded it on the rear floorboard.

"You're late," he clipped, already in reverse.

Her wet hair framed her face as she angled her head to buckle the seatbelt and it triggered a fluttering in his chest. The visual reminded him of the days she'd spent by his hospital bed.

"I overslept."

"That doesn't seem like you."

"Don't presume to know me solely based on our working relationship." Tucking a damp lock of hair behind her ear, she went on. "We hardly know each other."

"I'm hopeful this trip will change that."

Dayton understood all that was amiss between them couldn't be solved in a two-day trip, but he hoped it would set them on the right course; and, somewhere in the back of his mind, he hoped it gave Reynolds time to figure out where the Sanders boy had gone. Likely, he was somewhere remote, laying low in the foothills of Montana or hiding among Olympic National's hemlocks, living free of consequence.

No further words were exchanged between Kenna and himself until they'd conquered 10 miles of interstate.

He nodded to a sign indicating a rest stop a mile ahead. "Would you like to drive a sports car for the first time?"

She scoffed. "And kill us both? No, thank you."

"Suit yourself. You know, we could have fun together, you and I, if you were receptive to it."

Despite her protest, he pulled off at the rest stop, if only to rile her. He threw the car in park and looked at her expectantly, offering her the keys.

Gently, she pushed his hand away. "I'm not really interested in us having any kind of fun together."

"Why not?" He leaned into her, their faces inches apart, but she did not recoil. Rain battered the windshield. "I want to have fun with you, laugh with you, cry with you. I want to die with you, Kenna, and I won't stop until you want the same things."

"Are you sure you're not psychotic?"

Her warm breath tickled Dayton's lips and it was pure madness to endure their proximity without ensnaring her in a kiss. He was of the opinion that the last thing she wanted was his lips on hers and so he opted for a safer point of contact. His fingers threaded through her hair and he brought his mouth to the shell of her ear.

"No, darling, that's love. The greatest emotional disturbance known to mankind."

Kenna

The car door slammed and the rain continued to fall and Kenna was alone, briefly, with her racing thoughts and flittering pulse. Dayton was gone but his scent lingered in the cabin. That strange mint cologne. She remembered his breath on her skin, his whisper in her ear, and her toes curled as a familiar heat pooled low in her stomach.

He returned to the running car with drenched hair. Glancing over his shoulder, he backed out of the space.

"It's freezing out there."

"I'll bet," she quietly conceded.

She fought against noticing how handsome he was in his dark jeans, the way his Patagonia fleece hugged his torso. The black curtain of hair falling across his cheek. She needed a distraction lest she stare at him the entire trip. Reaching for the media interface, she wavered, "Do you mind?"

"Please."

After fiddling with the touchscreen, she managed to find the Bluetooth function that connected to Dayton's phone. She didn't know what she expected to fill the airwaves, but the sweet strumming and lilting yet grating vocals of Cohen's *Suzanne* wasn't it. She served him a pained look.

"I sincerely hope you have something besides Leonard Cohen on your playlist. I can hardly listen to him for one song, let alone on a loop for a two-hour trip."

"His worst stuff is miles better than that hipster folk stuff you listen to. I'm convinced you exclusively listen to those chain coffee shop soundtracks."

Kenna jammed a finger into the arrow on the screen and her breath caught in her chest as the next title populated. "Greta van Fleet? I love them."

"Kiszka's vocals are wild. Pure artistry."

Amusement tugged at her lips. "It's funny you like them. Some people might refer to their sound as hipster folk."

His attention fell to her and though she should have been concerned that, for those few seconds, he wasn't watching the road, she was concerned only with the honeyed fire dancing in the black pits of his eyes. As Dayton returned his focus to the interstate, the lines framing his mouth creased.

"God." The single syllable rode the coattails of his exhalation.

"What?"

"You're even more beautiful when you're smug. How is that?"

Kenna turned toward the window to hide the pink creeping over her cheeks, willing herself to forget all of the reasons her heart slammed against her chest.

She was heading downstate with her boss to meet his family and he was paying her compliments and he was perverse, a little violent even, but she had gotten in the car with him anyway. The implications behind that choice were too dark for her weary mind to explore. Slowly, her eyes shut and the rhythm of her breathing lulled her to sleep.

Her stomach dropped as they edged into the driveway. A black Toyota with Utah plates was parked ahead of them, which she assumed was Carmen's rental car.

"I'll get the bags."

The trunk was already open and Kenna was too busy staring at the house to protest. A charming two-story with cedar shake siding painted a shade of green so light, it could've easily been mistaken for beige. A porch swing. Manicured shrubs lined the walkway. There was a garden of azaleas not unlike the one in Dayton's yard, and their blooms were the same shade. It was shockingly normal and, while it defied her expectations, the iron gates and gargoyles she had pictured would have been too on the nose.

"Where are your parents?" she asked, shutting the car door. Dead leaves crunched beneath their feet as they headed toward the porch steps.

"Doing whatever it is retirees do. It'll be well after six before they're home. Carmen told me they're dropping off supplies at the church for the holiday."

Lingering on the second step, she looked up at him where he stood on the landing. "I guess I don't understand why you wanted to leave so early, given that they won't be home all day."

"I wanted us to spend some time with my sister before we throw my parents into the mix, and I'd like to show you the house." His lips parted as he surveyed the suburban landscape. "I worry that you might be uncomfortable once they arrive."

She climbed the remaining steps.

"Why would you say that?"

It was then she noticed the screen door guarding the more decorative one, and she thought it was a strange design choice. Staring at the mesh, thoughts that were far from voluntary swarmed her. The smack of that same door hitting its frame back on the farm as she and her sisters migrated in and out of the house, dawn to dusk. Lugging baskets of apples to the porch until her arms burned as if they'd been set on fire. Her mother ducking her head out to call them in for a meal.

Most of the memories from her first 18 years of life were better off forgotten. It allowed a more crucial truth to click into place. The house may have held some key to further understand him. And that promise, however small, was worth the risk.

A whining erupted from the screen door.

His hand froze on the doorknob as he sighed, something he rarely did. "My parents don't necessarily agree with what you're aspiring to do. Nor do they care for the type of medicine I practice."

He went into the house and she followed suit, her chance to reply dying as they stepped over the threshold. The smell hit

Kenna right away. Something warm and sweet. Bananas and cinnamon. A repetitious beeping sounded within the home competing with a woman's voice.

"*Ay dios mio*, I torched the son of a bitch."

Dayton chuckled softly beside her, setting their bags in the foyer. "That would be my sister."

Heart in her throat, she trailed behind him toward the kitchen. As they drew closer, the warm, sweet smell faded and was replaced by something more akin to burnt bread. A woman with long, straight black hair pressed buttons on the oven while fanning the contents of a loaf pan. She spoke with her back to them.

"Great. Mom's going to ring my neck, or force me to remake it. I'd prefer the strangulation, to be honest."

"Carmen," Dayton said.

There was a pointed edge to his tone.

Spinning around to face them, she zeroed in on Kenna. She wore a black t-shirt dusted with flour. A sleeve of stained glass tattoos covered the entirety of her left arm. Her eyes were just like her brother's, hauntingly depthless pools of black. Though they shared the same hair color and were of similar stature, it didn't take long to deduce that they were fraternal rather than identical twins. The tip of her nose was small and delicate where his was sharp. Her jaw was angular while his was soft. Subtle differences set them apart.

"Carmen, this is Kenna."

She didn't mind the plainness of the introduction. It was better than being introduced as his administrative assistant or worse yet his girlfriend. Though she was inordinately nervous to be meeting any of Dayton's family, she forged a brave front, extending a hand. "Hello."

Carmen looked at her brother and laughed, a rich, throaty sound that filled the room. Ignoring the offered hand, she pulled Kenna in tight.

"We hug in this house."

Citrus and floral perfume suffused the air. It was difficult to believe the two of them were related. Dayton's sister was warm and welcoming yet she was hard-pressed to think of a time when he'd hugged her.

Had he ever done such a thing?

She braced her hands on Kenna's shoulders. A dark freckle marked her left cheekbone, a lone spot amid the unblemished canvas of her face.

"Do you bake at all? I could really use a second opinion. Our mom's a bit of a type A perfectionist so there's a good chance her head will explode if I mess this up."

A trained eye or nose wasn't required to reveal the bread's fate. "It's a little charred."

"Fuck, I knew it." Carmen turned the pan upside down and shook it over the trash until the loaf fell out. Preheating the oven, she mumbled, "At least I have time to remake it."

"Try baking it 10 minutes less, Betty Crocker. I'm going to take our stuff upstairs," Dayton said.

Kenna wandered out of the kitchen, surveying the main area of the house. Everything was light, neutral, and tasteful, from the walls to the drapes to the furniture. A collection of antique brass tools stood beside the fireplace. Crystal coasters. Gold-framed oil paintings. Those minor touches of elegance, while understated, raised questions. Dayton had scarcely relayed anything to her about his upbringing.

"Mom doesn't want you guys sharing a room," Carmen called out.

"I'm 39 years old."

"Just throwing it out there, brother."

He grabbed their bags and cast her a flicker of a smile as he started scaling the carpet runner stairs. "It's childish, but I was looking forward to holding you."

She hated that those words, coupled with their imagery, had

the power to clench her heart. More disturbing was the fact that Kenna wanted to be held by him. She longed to be wrapped in his arms, burrowed in his chest.

Slowly, it would heal him.

Their love, a light amid all of the dark that shadowed his existence. At that thought, her heart clenched for a different reason. She subconsciously referred to love in the plural and, though it was a small distinction, it sent her mind whirling.

An iciness enveloped her chest as she realized that some miniscule though irrefutable fraction of herself loved him.

She had fallen for the dark doctor.

Watching Dayton trot down the stairs in his snug-fitting denim, she swallowed. Her embarrassment made little sense. He was a psychiatrist, not a mind reader, yet she wondered if he heard the thumping of her pulse or detected the blood rushing to her cheeks.

It was closer to eight when the Merinos came through the front door in a cacophony of laughter and half-completed sentences. Dayton and Kenna sat as far away from each other as the confining love seat allowed. The arrangement was largely due to her fear that any kind of affection with him would further alter her already traitorous neural pathways. Carmen sprawled out on the larger sofa, a cable knit blanket draped over her legs.

Light and shadow danced against the walls as the fire crackled in the hearth. Carmen entertained them with tall tales from her job, most of which Dayton had already heard but he laughed on cue. The trio's conversation halted as the owners of the residence emerged in the sitting room.

A strand of pearls wreathed his mother's neck. She wore a pale pink blouse and khaki pants, and she carried a sack of takeout whose smell had already permeated the room. Overzealous quantities of garlic and butter. His father was similarly dressed and carried an identical sack.

"Eddy, did you remember we had a son?" his mother teased. Her forehead creased as a slow, subtle smile bloomed while regarding Kenna. "Oh, hello." And then Dayton. "Who's this, dear?"

His hand brushed her spine. She took the hint and rose with him, soon standing toe to toe with the people responsible for giving life to the man who had wreaked havoc on hers since they crossed paths.

"This is Kenna."

"A beautiful name for a beautiful young woman." His mother employed a less crushing embrace than Carmen had. "Gwendolyn. Call me Gwen. I insist."

His father tucked her in a one-armed side hug. "And I'm Edward, but I prefer Eddy. I hope we didn't keep you all waiting too long."

"Pleasure to meet you both," Kenna said.

She detested how shy the situation had rendered her and she felt like any of the other girls. Under his thumb, helpless.

Dayton exchanged hugs with his parents. Eddy's weathered hand cradled the back of his son's head and he examined his face.

"What happened to you, *mijo*?"

It took her all of one second to realize the question was in reference to his scars.

"Nothing serious."

Though she wasn't sure how long he'd had the scars, the fragment of conversation implied he had not been home since the car accident. Even more curiously, Dayton seemed to not want his parents to know about the crash.

Kenna noticed Carmen avert her eyes as her brother brushed off the severity of what he'd endured, and she fiddled with a frayed end of the blanket. She must have known. They were twins; it was probably encoded in their DNA to relay everything that happened to one another.

She had never wanted to be alone so badly with someone whom she knew so little.

But Gwen's smooth voice cut above the rest, killing her chance to pull Carmen aside and suss out whatever she obviously knew.

"Let's eat. Shall we?"

20
THE MERINOS

Kenna

*J*t was both thrilling and terrifying to be huddled around the table with Dayton's family, perfect strangers, praying over a meal.

Yet despite the air of unfamiliarity, the scene brought Kenna great comfort. It conjured memories of her own family murmuring grace before diving into whatever meal they'd managed to scrape together. Though not always desirable, they had always had food on their table, whatever game her father managed to trap. Her mother cleaned and prepared the meat.

Roasted grouse. Honey-glazed rabbit.

Everything tasted like chicken after a while.

The dining room was cozier than she'd expected. Their six-top table filled most of the space. An oxblood rug stretched beneath their feet. Taper candles burned to near nubs provided an intimate wash of light. Gwen and Carmen had transferred all of the dishes into serving bowls, which they presently passed around the table as everyone filled their plates.

"What time did you two get in?" Gwen asked.

"Around noon," Dayton said, handing off a bowl of marsala to Kenna without sparing her a look.

A 'v' formed between her graying brows. "Ah. We were at the volunteer clinic."

"You guys are still doing that?"

"A couple of days a week. It's nice to have something to keep you busy when your own flesh and blood seldom grace you with a visit."

Carmen aimed her fork at Gwen. "Hey, I visit."

"We know you do, Carmina," Eddy cut in. He was a fading version of his son, still elegantly handsome despite the fact that he was getting on in age, and spoke with the faintest whisper of a dying accent. "Your brother, on the other hand."

Dayton released a tired sigh, looking from his plate to his parents. "I know it's been a long time. I have no excuse."

Another sigh. He'd had no shortage of those since they arrived in Eugene. It seemed he had little patience for his family. She found his behavior around them rather amusing.

An intimidating doctor reduced to a little boy.

Gwen sipped her wine, muttering, "Too busy with your heathen science, I suppose."

Kenna's skin tightened beneath her sweater as his warning from the porch sank in. His parents rejected anything relating to mental health. No wonder his visits were scarce. It was, in fact, the same reason she hadn't been home to see her own family; but they didn't simply reject her career aspirations, they rejected the idea of post-secondary education altogether.

"What is it you do, Kenna?" Eddy asked. His expression was warm, welcoming. Eyes a golden brown. The twins had inherited their mother's eyes.

Dark and cold.

She resolved to skirt around the precise answer as long as possible. "I'm in my first year of grad school."

He prompted further. "What do you study?"

"Heathen science."

"I wasn't aware Ponderosa had a medical school." Gwen frowned, nearly mirroring Dayton's words the first time they met.

"They don't. I'm a psychology major. Truthfully, I don't think I have the stamina for med school."

"Not everyone does," she conceded. "The three of us made it, somehow."

Carmen stared into her plate, her bare face unreadable. Kenna almost dropped her fork from the thought alone of sitting around a table with not one but three doctors, even if two of them were retired.

Dayton took a long pull from his glass of water. He was the only one not drinking wine. She thought he might have had a glass, given the acute stress he appeared to be under, but Gwen had prepared everyone's drinks. Though his mother didn't support his career, she at least seemed adamant about protecting his cardiovascular condition. Then again, Kenna couldn't determine if that was a byproduct of being a loving mother or a doctor.

Carmen covered her mouth as she chewed around a bite of food. "So, where are you from, kid?"

"Don't call her that," Gwen chided. "She's a grown woman."

"It's fine," Kenna said.

And it was. While Dayton and Carmen's voices were far from the same pitch, they sounded identical when they said the word. She focused only on Carmen's face. It was open, inviting, as if she genuinely wanted to know Kenna, and it imbued her with the courage to drop details she hadn't ever spared Dayton.

"New York. I grew up on a farm. An apple orchard, actually. My grandparents were first-generation immigrants. They passed the orchard down to my dad."

"It sounds like you had an enriching childhood," Eddy said. "Living off the land. Now, that's the way to live. Instilled a good work ethic in you, too, I'd imagine."

"My five sisters and I stayed busy."

Dayton turned to her, face flush with pure astonishment. "You have *five* sisters?"

Sipping her wine, Kenna shrugged.

"Six daughters. Bless your mother's heart. I commend her, truly. I wouldn't have survived such a tremendous feat." Gwen laughed. "I don't mean to be presumptuous, please correct me if I'm wrong, but, given your name, I assume that your grandparents immigrated from Ireland?"

She easily masked her offense. "Yes."

"Were you raised Catholic, then?"

"I was, and I still attend church."

Gwen let out a stilted 'hah' and steepled her hands. "I've prayed for so long that Dayton would find a good, Catholic girl." She raised her glass and stared down her son. "Here's to hoping you can keep this one."

The remainder of dinner passed by without much event. It was a calm, quiet affair. No drama, scandal, or secret spilled. Gwen tasked Dayton with the dishes. Once everyone had gone their separate ways to their rooms, Kenna found him stationed at the farmhouse sink, which looked out of place in the outdated kitchen. The sleeves of his henley were pushed just above his elbows. An apple fragrance hung heavy in the air, the noxious plume of the dish soap. His phone sat off to the side of the drying rack where Sam Cooke's velvety voice crooned at a low volume.

There was hope for his taste in music yet.

"Do you need help?"

"Who do you suppose washes the dishes at my house?"

There was something softer about Dayton. His tone, his expression; she couldn't place it. Perhaps it was the day's exhaustion paired with the familiarity of being in his childhood home. Kenna could've grown attached to this version of him but she didn't allow it. His altered demeanor would not follow them home to Branch Spring, where the enigma of Dr. Dayton Merino would reign free.

She watched him work, admiring the veins straining against the top sides of his hands and the gentle manner in which he placed the china into the drying rack, like he didn't want to chance waking the rest of the household who were almost certainly still awake.

In a hushed voice, she sang along to *You Send Me* and he beheld her with a fondness that gave the impression the domestic backdrop was their own.

"Are you still playing …" He didn't dare mention the bar by name. Was it remorse on his end or was he avoiding stirring up her feelings regarding Lacey's death? She would've given the world to know. "Downtown?"

"Every once in a while. Mostly at Striker Lounge."

"The converted warehouse on 15th Street?"

"That's the one."

The song changed and their chatter faded. The whole affair had a hypnotic effect on her; the sponge crushed beneath his hand, the running water and clink of porcelain. Hypnosis was an impermanent state. For all the normalcy he exuded in that scene, he was the furthest thing from it.

"Why don't you head upstairs. Get ready for bed. I put your stuff in my old room."

Kenna turned without a word and retreated up the staircase. She enjoyed the simple commands from Dayton, and that was when she suspected she'd fallen helplessly for him: following them without any thought or hesitation.

Contented, even, to do so.

She wondered how it was possible to conceive of loving him, knowing what she did. Love often made little sense.

There were five shut doors on the second floor. Light pooled out from the bottom of one and she assumed it was Carmen's. The first bedroom Kenna came across was tidy and generic in design, indicative of use for guests. She spotted Dayton's bag by the nightstand as she switched off the light. She tried her luck on the other side of the hallway, where she was duped by a linen closet, and then a bathroom before finding herself in Dayton's old bedroom.

His green and white Sheldon High lacrosse jersey was pinned to the wall above the dresser. She slid open the top drawer enough to glimpse its contents. Full of clothes, like he'd never left. A short stack of books sat atop the dresser, the selection varying wildly from the strictly non-fiction collection Dayton kept back in Branch Spring. Her fingers ghosted along the spines. Michael Crichton. Nick Hornby.

She pulled them away before grazing the Thomas Harris that rested at the bottom.

A CD player occupied the opposite end of the dresser, albums lining the space between the player and the books.

"You don't waste any time."

Her hand flew to her chest but she recovered quickly as Dayton closed the door behind him and was soon capable of producing coherent speech.

She took in his overgrown hair and dark eyes, the lips that had once kissed every inch of her skin. In spite of their fraught history and the newfound affection she harbored for him, she understood that some degree of danger lay in choosing to love him.

The longer Kenna looked at him, the more confused she became as to why, all of a sudden, a large part of her insisted that the threat didn't matter.

Dayton

"Did you mean what you said earlier? In the car?"

Her eyes were wider than usual, as if accommodating their earnestness. Kenna was like a piece of glass before him. He saw straight through her, vulnerability and fragility on display. That piercing look tugged at something buried deep within Dayton's chest.

He wouldn't deny her an answer.

"I've never said anything more genuine. To anyone."

Saying nothing, she returned her focus to the CDs. He doubted she was studying the titles but rather it acted as a convenient focal point for her to gather her thoughts while she couldn't bear to look at him.

He approached her from behind, encircling his arms around her. Though he felt Kenna's ribs hitch, she didn't protest at the proximity. In that moment, he caught a glimpse of what their romantic relationship might entail—were they to ever fall into one. Breathing exercises for her to stomach their intimacy and a vicious cycle of establishing small doses of trust before some discovery on her part inevitably eroded it.

She pulled out *Almost in Love*. "Elvis?"

"He got all the girls."

"So do you." Her words stung, but he didn't let their venom linger. She replaced the CD, her hands covering his. "Why me? Why not any of the others?"

It was a fair question and yet Dayton found himself unable to say any of the things streaming through his mind. There had never been an endgame so to speak with any of the girls. By the same token, none of them had asserted themselves quite like Kenna had. That entire semester, he'd schemed to have her and she'd schemed against him and they slowly, accidentally became something to each other they didn't know they needed. While he still wasn't sure *what* they were, he knew that he loved her and couldn't fathom letting her go.

"I don't know. Somewhere along the way you became important. The more time we spent together ... I knew."

"Knew what?" she whispered.

Heartbeat quickening, he dared to speak the words on the tip of his tongue. He'd no longer hold them back. "That I wanted you. Only you. Forever."

Gathering her hair, he put it to one side and placed open-mouthed kisses on the nape of her neck. She reached back and pulled his own hair, as if his lips could get any closer, could delve past the skin and into the ribbons of nerves and delicate vertebrae that lay beneath. He would've done it, if he could.

Kenna gasped as his tongue traced her spine and she freed his hair in favor of clutching the dresser. Hands sliding lower, he unzipped her jeans and tugged them down the subtle curves of her hips. He touched her like he'd never again have the chance. His palms roved over her thighs, up to her waist, under her shirt where he inched along her stomach and finally let his hand rest on her chest, wrist pinned between her breasts. Whatever precious little autonomy he had left was broken. Her body ruled him.

Though Dayton heard her quickening breath and felt her pounding heart, he yearned for proof that she wanted this as much as he did.

Fingers fanning out over her chest, he clutched at her skin as if it were fabric and she released a sigh that was so uninhibited, pure yet erotic, that he yanked her underwear and sent them falling to her ankles. She made no motion to stop him but mumbled something akin to 'lock the door.' The request was lost on his ears. Everything was muted with her silken skin beneath his fingertips.

She was the only thing in existence.

How glorious it was to caress her tender flesh once more. He'd spent many nights alone equipped with nothing but memories and the three pictures of her he had in his possession. Truthfully, that had been when he'd known she was his forever—though he'd suspected as much at Nathan's wedding. Reliving the experience had satiated him with all of Kenna's predecessors, but revisiting the lone night she'd spent in his bed spawned lunacy closely trailed by the regret of having driven her away.

"Should I ..." Her timid question faded, unasked, as she hiked one her legs onto the low dresser. The sight was almost his undoing. Leaning over wearing nothing but a t-shirt.

She arched her back as he pushed into her. He savored it all. The quiet cries of pleasure tumbling from her lips, the perfume emanating off her neck.

Oh, the perfume.

He had to draw her body nearer, the vanilla, that comforting smell. Dayton held her still with one hand, burying the other in her hair, tugging on it to bring them closer.

"Dayton," she breathed his name and it was pure bliss.

Her voice. Her heat.

He moved within Kenna, gritting his teeth, thinking of how reluctant he'd be to surrender his hold on her when this was over. He never wanted to turn her loose. Her freedom was his insecurity. One day, she may decide she didn't want him. Everything they could be. When, and if, that day came, he would follow her and bring her back to where she belonged.

In his arms.

Brushing his lips against her temple, he mumbled, "Tell me you'll never leave, lamb. Promise."

She said nothing and, as his movement within her turned more desperate, he wondered if he'd spoken too softly or not at all.

21
NO REST FOR THE WICKED

Kenna

*A*fter Dayton had claimed her as his nightcap, Kenna switched on her phone's flashlight and turned the entire bedroom upside down in search of anything that might have been the least bit incriminating.

She had not found a thing, and though she was disappointed at coming up empty-handed, she slept easier.

Her heart was lodged in her throat as she carefully descended the stairs the following morning. Facing his family initially had been nothing short of anxiety-inducing, and Kenna predicted it would be nightmarish given their illicit activities once the evening had faded to dark.

As her hand curled around the railing and she drew closer to the main floor, she expected the familiar feeling of regret to weigh down her limbs. That leaden despair.

Quite the contrary. She felt light, as if her bones had become feathers overnight, and she practically glided across the hardwood when she reached the landing.

Muted sunlight streamed through the windows.

The wooden blinds were drawn. The drapes, tucked aside and tied off with neat bows. Someone else was awake.

A tea kettle squealed within the kitchen. Kenna was surprised to find Carmen, rather than her brother, at the source of the sound. Her glossy hair crowned her head in an enormous messy bun. A sweatshirt concealed her tattoos.

She turned off the gas burner and a slow smile spread across her face upon realizing she was no longer alone.

Reaching for a second mug, she asked, "Tea drinker?"

"I've learned to make do."

The featherlight feeling dissipated and Kenna grew uncertain about the response. She wasn't sure what Dayton had told her about their relationship, or lack thereof. It was something she should've thought to inquire about amid the stifled moans and lip biting.

Tea in tow, they settled in the living room. A fire blazed, its steady crackling the only relief during an uncomfortable period of silence in which Carmen stared at her while they intermittently sipped from their mugs. Her intensity was reminiscent of her brother's but there was a softness to her gaze that was rarely seen in his.

"Did he come down?" Kenna finally asked.

"Went for a run."

"It's sprinkling."

Carmen's brows flexed in disapproval.

"Dayton would run in a thunderstorm." Coyness pulled at her lips. "And while we're on the topic of things that are dangerous and stupid, I heard you two *breathing* last night. The walls are paper thin in our house."

Shame flayed her from within.

"I'm sorry we subjected you to that."

We. It singed her tongue.

While they'd been intimate twice and she'd concluded that she loved Dayton, the idea alone of entering any kind of relationship with him was the very pinnacle of disaster.

Carmen fiddled with the tag dangling from the lip of her mug. "Usually, I'm protective of my brother. I barely know you but I feel like I need to be a little protective of you too."

She continued to glance at the windows looking out onto the front porch, worried that Dayton may have reappeared without warning.

"He's been pretty vague about you two, so I don't know if you're serious or not but, the thing is, he *never* brings anyone home, so. You seem like a nice enough kid and I just feel like I should warn you." Blowing out a concentrated line of breath, she shook her head and mumbled to herself, "After what happened with Audrey."

Bumps rose on Kenna's forearms at the casual namedrop. Was it the same Audrey whom Dayton had referred to when he'd assisted her with the trauma project? She felt certain of the answer before the question had halfway formed in her mind.

"He's cheated in every relationship he's been in. Not that there have been many. And I'm not just talking about one time. He'd cheat multiple times, always with different people, and then he'd call me and treat me like a 24-hour confessional."

Carmen laughed but it was devoid of humor.

"I had no idea."

"He means well. At least, I think he does." She paused, searching for the right words. "But it's like there's this part of himself he can't control, no matter how hard he tries. He's my twin. I should side with him, no matter what, but … you said you're in graduate school so I'm sure you have a hell of a lot going on in your life right now. You don't need heartbreak thrown into the mix." Carmen's eyes brimmed with something she couldn't quite place. "Just be careful with him, for both your sake."

The front door creaked inward on its hinges as Dayton came into the house, muddy tennis shoes dangling from two fingers. He didn't acknowledge Kenna in the slightest but he glanced at his sister while heading toward the stairs. "They're expecting us in 30. You two better change."

Her chest sank at the steps creaking under his weight.

Had he not declared her his forever before fucking her against a dresser some 12-odd hours earlier?

Maybe it had all been an elaborate dream.

"No rest for the wicked." Mug in hand, Carmen swept toward the stairs. "C'mon, kid. If we're late they'll never let us forget it."

Kenna registered what day it was, along with the absence of the smell of meat roasting in the oven.

"Late for what?" she managed, getting to her feet.

"The soup kitchen. It's tradition. Our mom always used to say, 'How can we eat Thanksgiving dinner while Eugene's going hungry?' When we were little—"

"Don't tell that story, Caramello." Dayton's objection echoed from upstairs.

Caramello. Carmina. Carmen.

Everyone in the house had a different name for her.

She lowered her voice and went on with it despite her brother's protest. "When we were little, 6 or 7, we stayed with our aunt while our parents volunteered at the soup kitchen. We were helping set the table and Dayton starts shaking his head and goes, 'I wish mom and dad could eat with us. Eugene should learn to cook for himself.'"

Kenna stifled a laugh and suddenly it was easy to picture him as a kid. Young, uninhibited.

Shirtless and unamused, Dayton looked down upon them from the second-floor landing. "I hope you've already showered. I'm not sparing you an ounce of hot water after your deliberate betrayal."

They saw Eddy and Gwen for 10 seconds when they arrived at St. Mary's, long enough for them to greet each other before heading off to their separate stations. Gwen snagged Carmen against her will as an extra set of hands in the church's kitchen. Kenna and Dayton were assigned to the small group of people serving food.

A most foul delight spread through her chest as he helped her out of her coat. His own sister had given her a warning of which she was already well aware.

Yet despite every piece of evidence and testimony that advised against it, Kenna loved him. Even if she never told him.

What good would come of such a revelation?

Yes, he claimed to mirror those feelings but she suspected she was nothing more to him than an entertaining pitstop on his twisted map of lovers that was destined to stretch far beyond their involvement.

She zoned out on a pair of volunteers who were unfolding disposable tablecloths and draping them over the tables, wholly transfixed on the billowing sheets of PVC. Something slapped in her hands and the trance was broken. Her pulse banged around her body like a pinball at full speed as she and Dayton slipped on the suggested but not required plastic gloves.

"So, is this part of the reason you don't like coming home?" she asked.

"No. I don't mind this." His neck tensed, cords popping against that rigid column. "The lack of medical discourse bothers me. I have doctors for parents and they'd sooner broach the subject of religious and civil unrest in the Middle East than dare to discuss our work."

"That must be hard for you."

It was the same detached, clinical dialogue she'd heard Dayton use ad nauseam with his patients. It worked just as well here. She lacked a better response.

He shrugged.

"They think psychiatrists have a God complex, that people should go to church instead of my office. They're my parents. I should see them more often, but it's hard to get past their dismissal of the very thing I went through 12 years of schooling and residency for. The thing that I'm proud to do."

Tentatively, Kenna reached out and touched his wrist. "I value the work you do. It's tremendously important. I'm sorry your parents don't see that."

His smile was weak but present.

Her ringtone sounded among the pile of coats and bags in the corner. She'd forgotten to put it on silent. She reflexively pressed ignore as the screen proclaimed *Home*.

"Your family?" he surmised.

If Dayton wanted her to be his forever—as much as she was disinclined to believe those words—she supposed it was best for him to get acquainted with the ugliness of the life she'd left behind. "I gave up trying to talk to them a while ago."

"None of them? Not even your sisters?"

"It's not like any of them have cell phones, and our parents screen every incoming call so I'd have to deal with one of them before I'd be allowed to talk to any of my sisters."

A cool, calculated moment passed before he spoke.

"It's hard to believe you grew up that way, off the grid. You're incredibly well-adjusted."

"As well-adjusted as someone who had to run away to attend college can be, I guess."

His lips parted as if to reply but he was cut off by a man in baggy jeans and a black hooded sweatshirt. "Dayton Merino's still in the Emerald City. Well, I'll be damned."

An older woman setting up trays and utensils at the end of the service line shot him a look of disbelief.

"Sorry, Ms. Patterson."

"It isn't me you owe an apology, boy."

He signed the cross while rolling his eyes and Kenna silently took offense to the stranger's overt juvenility.

"Just visiting." Dayton made no move to ask him how he was

doing and he didn't bother introducing her—though she believed the lack of introduction was a small kindness.

"You play in college? Guess not after your accident. We had a killer season the year after you quit. Good to know you're still around. Some of us thought you'd ..." He made a crackling sound and swiped at his neck. "Heart's still beating. That's something to be thankful for today, eh?"

"Truly a blessing," Dayton deadpanned.

Under normal circumstances, Kenna would've laughed at his seldom seen brand of humor but she was lost in the terrifying implication behind what his friend had said.

His thumb brushed his scraggly, blonde facial hair. "And hey, it's alright about Nicole. We both know she was a slut anyway."

"Son, your profanity isn't welcome here." Ms. Patterson narrowed her eyes; whether it was out of annoyance or a byproduct of poor vision was unclear.

"Nice seeing you."

"Yeah, you too." Dayton waited until he was out of earshot before speaking again. "That was Zach. We played lacrosse together."

"I gathered that much."

"Go on."

Tilting her head to one side, she frowned.

"Aren't you going to ask about Nicole? In keeping with your adorable mission to uncover every sin I've committed."

"Actually, no." Kenna had no interest in whoever this Nicole person was. Zach's comment about his health, however, was eating her alive.

People started trickling through the service line. She offered a portion of mashed potatoes and a polite smile between whispered comments to Dayton.

"What was he talking about? You told me your condition wasn't serious, that you weren't *dying*."

He stared straight ahead into the bustling refectory, rather than at her, when he replied, "We're all living on borrowed time, kid."

It took all she had to bite back a laugh.

"I let your sister get away with calling me that but that doesn't mean you get a free pass. And I thought we were long past evading each other's questions."

The service line grew busier and cut their conversation short. Her heartbeat echoed in her ears as she carried out the repetitive process. Scoop and smile. Finally, they were granted a brief reprieve as the tables filled up and fewer people came through the doors.

Flecks of pain lurked in Dayton's eyes.

"I'm not evading your question. I answered with a fact. We're all dying. Every one of us, minute by minute. Some of us just carry a greater risk of having our lives cut short."

Something beautifully tragic shifted in his face as he spoke this truth he seemed to fear. A shift occurred within Kenna too. Not quite the understanding she craved, but a most unexpected emotion. Empathy.

22

PROCEDURE

Dayton

Some kind of magic had transformed Kenna during their trip for when they returned she refused his offer to bring her back to her apartment.

She stayed with him.

He was determined to rectify the course off which their romantic potential had careened and it seemed things were heading in that direction.

Immense joy bloomed in his chest. He could've opened the window and belted out a musical number as they barreled down the interstate but he didn't want to arouse suspicion when her concerns had—for the meantime—subsided.

It was wonderful to bring her bag inside rather than leaving it in the trunk. She gave him an easy smile as he unlocked the door and he drank in the image of her standing on his doorstep, waiting to be let in, and he was infected with the dangerous, foolish hope that they would one day share his home. Even so, it was a hope he'd never set free.

"I thought your parents were sweet, aside from their selective belief in science and medicine." Kenna shimmied out of her coat and draped it across the arm of the couch. She sat, running a hand through her hair. "And I love Carmen."

Dayton had been more nervous to introduce her to his sister than to his parents. While Kenna had been by his side during one of his low points, Carmen had seen him at the absolute lowest. Again and again. When the three of them stood in the kitchen, his anticipation for their meeting had been so palpable, it electrified the air.

Leaving a hand's worth of space between them, he settled in beside her. "She was a big fan of you too."

She cast her eyes away from him, gaze falling to her lap, and he knew at once she had something pressing at the forefront of her mind.

One of her maddeningly beautiful quirks.

"She said she felt like she needed to protect me, to ... warn me." It wasn't a question in the traditional sense but the inquisition lay in Kenna's tone.

"And did she?"

"Somewhat."

His hand covered her thigh. She held her breath. Chest, unmoving. A doe in a clearing, frozen, vying for another day of life. Couldn't she see he'd laid his arms down long ago?

That he no longer posed a threat?

"Carmen and I have a unique relationship. We've always been exceptionally close, like most twins, I guess. We look out for each other. You have siblings, you must understand that to an extent."

Dayton wouldn't give her the satisfaction of answering whatever question she was skirting around.

Usually she was blunt, unafraid, the opposite of the woman sitting beside him, slowly nodding her head though clearly far off in a tangle of thoughts, as was her custom.

Kenna's brows drew together before her expression neutralized and she looked at him once more. It didn't require much effort to angle his head and capture her lips. He didn't hesitate as she widened her mouth, relishing the taste of the gas station coffee lingering on her sweet tongue.

Though it was clear she was working out a problem in her pretty little head, she wasn't repulsed by his lips, his tongue. She was conscious of every press, every sweep, and she acted alongside him, harmonizing.

But as his hand slipped toward her lower back, one of hers flew to it and her lids sprung open.

"Dayton, I have to tell you something."

His heart pounded for reasons that had nothing to do with their passion seconds earlier. The last time she'd interrupted a kiss to tell him something, she had revealed that she knew too much, discovered things he'd wished she'd never known, loving her as he did.

Love never came easy. There would always be obstacles to overcome and he could think of plenty in the reserves, waiting for their chance to attack.

With bated breath, he waited for gunfire.

Kenna

Nerves festered inside of her. She had wanted to reveal her feelings while they were in Eugene but she failed to pin down an appropriate moment.

But in the space where Kenna had forged bravery and had it shattered, it felt inexplicably right. She stared into Dayton's black pools, heartbeat accelerating as she considered her own reasoning for the forthcoming confession.

Was her love genuine or was the declaration another advancing pawn on the chessboard she thought they'd long abandoned? Even she wasn't sure.

He stared back, face neutral, chest rising and falling with the passing of tranquil breaths.

Her lips parted but an exhalation prevailed over speech.

The permanence of what was so close to sliding off her tongue shook her to the core. It was an admission neither of them would ever forget, and she couldn't decide if that was good or bad.

"Kenna?"

The sound was so soft she was sure she'd imagined it until she noticed his face was inclined toward hers, features laced with expectancy.

Her lips parted once more but a commotion outside stalled her thoughts. Heavy footsteps thundered on the porch followed by a knock infused with such authority it demanded an answer. More footsteps ensued. Muffled voices.

The door swung inward and Kenna grew faint as they stood face-to-face with a squadron of police officers, led by a lanky man in a dark suit. He presented a gold badge and the faint feeling escalated to a numbness that swirled through her body like novocaine.

"Detective Brian Reynolds with the Portland Police Bureau. I have a warrant from Branch Spring P.D. to search the premises."

"I know who you are."

"Procedure. Surely you know all about that, doc."

He whistled and the officers flooded through the front door like a gang of bloodhounds. They were everywhere all at once. The living room, the makeshift office, the kitchen, disappearing through the hallway and into the bedroom. The same over-whelming need to escape consumed her as it had the day she dared to look inside the box. Her supply of oxygen ceased, searing the underside of her lungs.

Was that why they had come?

Had they reviewed her report they'd initially laughed off and uncovered something worth investigating? She realized that hope was inspired by real love, the hope that she had landed Dayton in this situation and that he had not gone off and committed some heinous act.

Chills ghosted her limbs as she stood perfectly still and watched the officers rifle through drawers while others thumbed through papers. It was a scene ripped straight from one of her worst dreams and yet it unfolded in real time.

Seconds ticking in cadence with her pulse.

The detective's smooth-talking voice cured Kenna's state of shock. "I was more than a little disappointed when I saw your flashy car in the driveway. I prefer to conduct my searches while the resident is out. Just my luck."

Dayton was startlingly calm for someone who was having his house searched. Though, she supposed any other reaction would have drawn suspicion.

"There must be some kind of mistake," he said.

"Mistake isn't in my vocabulary. It was a stretch calling it probable cause, but I got my lieutenant behind it."

Detective Reynolds tore off his glasses and glanced at her, as if he was debating saying anything further with someone else in the room, but he hooked the glasses on the collar of his shirt and proceeded.

"Did you know there aren't any kind of surveillance cameras behind your practice? You don't have them, and neither do any of your neighboring renters. What, you guys never heard of break-ins? No use for security equipment in safe little East Haven?"

The ringing in her ears competed with the detective's words. Dayton and Kenna were intermediates at their metaphorical chess game but Reynolds was a grandmaster.

"I haven't been a tenant very long. I suppose I haven't really given much thought to having a system installed."

"Why don't we continue this conversation down at the station. Give my boys some space. They're a thorough bunch."

Producing a stiff nod, Dayton shot her an apologetic look and stepped outside. She couldn't stay while the warrant was being executed. That much was clear. The room spun as she grabbed her purse and she fought to stay upright while heading for the door. Detective Reynolds stuck out his foot, preventing her from slipping past him.

This close, Kenna noticed the pockmarks dotting his cheeks. The hair that had been combed more recently than it had been washed. He spoke low, extending a card toward her.

"Give me a call if you happen to know something."

Snatching the card, she hurried outside.

She lingered on the porch, shell-shocked, as Dayton and the detective got into a black SUV and disappeared down the street. A shiver crested over her, recalling the menacing edge in Reynolds' voice when he implored her to give him a call, and she worried that she'd end up as an accessory to a crime Dayton may or may not have committed. She did have a bank vault of information on him, after all.

Chest heaving, Kenna gripped the railing. Fear exhausted all of her systems, leaving her deep sense of panic nowhere to nest. The familiar heat of bile crept up her throat and she vomited all over the garden of eggshell and salmon azaleas, tears falling in tandem.

Once the spell passed, she squared her shoulders, ordered an Uber, and waited at the end of the driveway, never turning once to look at 673 Fairbrook.

Upon arriving at her apartment, she had to phone the superintendent to let her in after rummaging around in her purse for what felt like an hour for a set of keys that weren't there. She must have dropped them during her hasty getaway or mixed them in with her luggage.

Either way, her keys were at Dayton's place and she had no intention of returning after what the detective had implied.

The unit was dead silent with Liza still out of town and Kenna couldn't have been more grateful for that solace. The thought alone of processing her wild, competing emotions with anyone else around, even one person, had her bordering on mental collapse.

The 10 minutes she'd spent with Lacey Greene flashed through her head like a horror film. Her vacant stare out the window and the way she had slowly pivoted her head to meet their eyes. She covered her ears as if she actually heard the flickering film reel.

Weeks had passed since she'd revisited the files on her laptop but she could no longer ignore them. Detective Reynolds' divine timing had seen to that.

Staring back at her was information she had gone over countless times—she'd practically memorized it all—but one line of text in her notes stood out as if it had been underlined in red ink. *Audrey Dresden, UCLA, sexual acquaintance.*

Perhaps she wouldn't have zeroed in on the name otherwise but Carmen had mentioned it. What were the chances that Audrey never left Los Angeles?

Social media revealed 13 matches in L.A. and its surrounding areas but only one who'd graduated from UCLA. Her profile stated she was 37 and her location was marked Silver Lake. She had a pixie cut. Large, doe-like eyes. Kenna sent her a brief message, all the while imagining how expressive those same eyes would be while she sought answers to her tryst with Dayton.

Before Audrey had a chance to respond, she was browsing Greyhound routes, her in-case-of-emergency credit card at the ready. Under normal circumstances, she would've deemed traveling to Los Angeles a drastic measure.

But with the Portland Police Bureau insinuating that, perhaps, Dayton had something to do with Lacey's death, she had to get out of town. Out of state. She was tired of attempting to solve this puzzle that only grew more complicated as each new piece clicked into place.

Only the fact that the pieces were living, breathing, and aching in their incompleteness gave Kenna cause to push onward.

23
POOR GIRL

Dayton

*A*sking for a lawyer would've made him appear weak so he sat, mute, ready to cooperate only because he had no other choice.

A shoddy pendant light illuminated the interview room. Detective Reynolds sat across from him at the gunmetal table while Dayton stared at its surface. Different shades of gray comprised the interior, making for a morose atmosphere. A red light blinked in the upper left-hand corner.

Recording was in progress.

He'd once been thrown in jail for an entire day before Carmen came to his rescue, maxing out her platinum card to post his bail. This time, his wrists were unbound and he was treading new territory. Detained for interrogation.

Even if he did wind up in the same position, he was confident his sister wouldn't show up with a quarter of a million dollars and a loving embrace.

Murderers don't walk free.

"You know your Miranda rights?"

"Do I need to be Mirandized, detective?"

Reynolds snorted. "I don't really give a shit. You're in my house now. We're going to play by my rules. *Comprende?*"

He gave a fractional nod.

Dayton felt as though everything had been emptied out of him. Every time he got close to Kenna, something tore them apart; first, her discovery of the Polaroids, and now the search warrant. She was probably packing as he sat in the cool, empty room, preparing to flee and change her name and forget the deranged doctor who loved her. And, though it would be painful, he would let her.

Only in his absence would she blossom into who she was meant to be, no longer wilted by his affections.

Reynolds reclined in his chair with a casualness that reeked of egotism. "Things aren't looking good for you, *ese.*"

"Every officer employed by this station is currently tearing my home apart and I'm trapped in a room with a racist detective, so I'd say you're right. I am a natural-born citizen of this country. Not that you care."

"The other week when I paid you a visit, we only suspected that you may have been the last person to see Ms. Greene alive. We've reviewed the footage twice from the days preceding and following her disappearance, and we were able to confirm that you are *the* last confirmed person she was seen with. Which means she either disappeared into the wilderness, or—"

"What are you going to lay on me next? Surely, you didn't bring me in just to relay that."

"I corroborated your whereabouts the night of the murder. Your story conveniently checked out about the hospital. But," his lips curled into a predatory smile, "Owens-Adair is an old facility operating on outdated surveillance technology. Almost half the cameras are blacked out around the building, some of which cover the parking lot."

"I was there the entire time. I went straight to my shift at the hospital from my practice, just as I told you before."

Reynolds put forth no argument but served him a hard stare. He wanted to witness Dayton crumble under the questioning, to be fearful at the very least. He wouldn't dare allow the detective that satisfaction.

"I didn't look into you before because Sanders and his sick little basement seemed the obvious route, but now? I want you for this, doctor, and when I want something, I get it." He slid something across the table that Dayton thought he'd never see again: his Los Angeles County mugshot. Hands clasped, he went on, "You've been arrested before. March 19, 2007. Why don't you tell me about that?"

The pain associated with the memory had dulled to the point of tolerance. While he'd loved Audrey, it didn't begin to compare to the way he felt about Kenna.

With Kenna, love was rendered an inadequate label, much more than a hollow word echoed between lovers.

It was a state of being, indescribable and invasive, like sunshine shooting through his veins, delivering warmth to every dark corner of his soul.

And that precious light that had long evaded him was one of many reasons he needed to keep his head screwed on around Detective Brian Reynolds, Portland Police Bureau.

"There's not much to tell. I was unfaithful and, as a result, we had a difference of opinion about the status of our relationship."

"So, you broke into her sorority with the hope that what? She'd take your sorry ass back?"

"It was a foolish thing to have done. I regret it to this day, and it made my residency interviews a living hell. I wasn't officially charged with anything but spending the night in jail doesn't look good when you're trying to impress a board of doctors."

Ignoring the anecdote, Reynolds pressed on with his assertions.

"Well, if romantic altercations get you fired up, that certainly puts the footage in a new light."

"Nothing romantic occurred between myself and Ms. Greene. I saw her only on two occasions."

Reynolds swung his feet up on the corner of the table, heels thunking against the metal. "No, I don't mean Lacey. That cute little redhead you're always running around with. Let me ask you something, Merino, is chaos woven into the fabric of your life or do you concoct this shit over your morning coffee? This poor girl went from being mentored by you to working for you to getting shunned and shamed at her own university *because* of you to—from what I can tell—serving as your plaything. And I'm thinking she must be your motivation, you know? You've gone to such lengths to control her, keep her in your life, and maybe somehow in that twisted brain of yours, what with your history of infidelity and all, you thought Lacey showing up might wreck everything. So you had to get rid of her. Because, lo and behold, who shows up for her shift less than 20 minutes after your interaction with Miss Lacey Greene? None other than your redhead."

"Tread lightly when you share your conspiracy theories with your lieutenant. I'd hate for you to lose your badge." His heartbeat rattled like a lone marble rolling around a 10-gallon barrel but Dayton leaned into the table and steeled his face. "The only thing I'm guilty of is being in the wrong place at the wrong time."

"Oh, you were there at the right time. I haven't connected all the dots yet but I will. Count on it."

The detective's chair screeched as he pushed away from the table. He rose and walked halfway to the door before turning to Dayton.

"You're free to go, you piece of shit. For now."

He called Kenna several times throughout the day once he

returned to his now destroyed home, but on each occasion it went straight to voicemail.

Either her phone was dead or she was manually ignoring his calls. Her silence paired with the detective's hour-long mindfuck interrogation had him restless, like an animal confined to a cage that was much too small. He couldn't get away from himself, thoughts circling, urging him to succumb to the madness with which he was so familiar. *No.* His pacing halted as he tore at his hair.

He'd resolved to put his malevolence behind him.

All of the mistakes he had made had trained him in a way, strengthening his resolve so as not to stray from Kenna, that brightly burning light guiding him out of a lifetime of darkness. But he wasn't entirely out of the dark.

Lacey was dead and the investigators were cracking under the pressure of making an arrest, evident in Detective Reynolds' repeated questions and the deep purple bags ringing his bloodshot eyes. Despite his false bravado, he'd seemed dissatisfied with where their interview had ended up, but Dayton knew better than to exhale. With the boyfriend having split town, he knew he was their secondary suspect.

If he so much as dipped his toes in the water of legal trouble, his medical license could be suspended.

Or revoked entirely.

He was sure he had done everything right so as not to draw suspicion to himself. The blasted traffic cameras erased that certainty. Video evidence existed of him and Lacey interacting. When the investigators inevitably came knocking, he had planned to tell them he had not associated with the Greene girl since their bizarre pseudo-session at the university. But Detective Reynolds turned up with his discovery and his smugness and cut down the innocence Dayton had prepared to feign. And yet, through it all— heart racing and head swimming—he maintained a relative calm during the rounds of questioning.

Standing still in his bedroom, his pulse ratcheted up once more as he considered the fact that the detective also knew he'd been at trivia with a former colleague the night the body was found. At the *venue* where it had been found.

He laughed without mirth. There perhaps had never been a series of circumstances as damning as the one in which he'd placed himself. His plan was working against him. Sanders had gone running, not him. And yet, somehow, Dayton was being sized up as the guilty party.

No aspect of his behavior was doing him any favors, neither the pacing nor the chasing rabbit holes. He had to get out of his house. Out of his mind.

Thumbing the two sets of keys in his pocket, he drew in a steadying breath and set out for Kenna's place.

Dayton spotted the Caprice as soon as he rounded the corner into the apartment complex parking lot.

Cutting the engine, he sat in silence, fixated on the stairs leading up to her shared unit. The station wagon's presence didn't mean she was there. Though, her robin's egg bike was chained up in its usual place as well and that seemed indicative of her presence.

His chest rose and fell as he idled in the driver's seat, the tranquility of his breath belying his inner panic.

In a surge of motion his hazy brain couldn't quite keep pace with, he was out of the car and climbing the stairs. Dayton raised a tight, confident fist and rapped on the door.

No response came and several impatient moments elapsed before he tried again. After three attempts, it became clear no one was home. He tore the keys out of his pocket and in one criminal twist found himself inside.

"Kenna?" he called out.

He was certain she wasn't there, but preferred to eliminate the chance that Liza was holed up in her room and had somehow not heard the earnest knocking.

The bathroom door, as well as the doors to both bedrooms, were all either halfway or wide open. All of the lights were off and the day's waning light streamed in through the eyelets of the plastic blinds. Momentarily, Dayton debated showing himself out. He had already committed so many wrongs.

What was one more?

Kenna's bedroom was nearest to the living room. This he knew only because she'd ducked in there to charge her phone during one of his infrequent visits.

His hand crept across the wall until it met the switch plate and light flooded the small space. Clothes littered the bed and floor. The closet door, ajar. It looked as if someone had ransacked the room in pursuit of valuables. A futile mission in the dwelling of broke college students.

Her laptop was open on her desk, its screen blackened. Dayton pushed the power button and was immediately greeted with her most recent activity. A confirmation for a Greyhound ticket. To Los Angeles.

The display turned his stomach, twisting and twisting until it sank and was just as swiftly replaced by a feeling of emptiness. Kenna's having left had not conjured the visceral reaction but rather the implication packed into her destination.

Who she had gone to meet.

A quiet rage welled within as he shut the laptop in one fluid motion. Carmen must have said something to her. There was no other explanation, no—

Dayton stilled his breathing. The front door opened.

"Kenna?" another voice called out.

Liza.

He pushed back from the desk with a nonchalance that suggested he lived there and had not let himself in with a conveniently misplaced set of keys.

There was a smacking sound in the other room.

"Oh my God. We have *no* food in the fridge. Didn't you get back a couple of days ago? What have you been eating? You've probably been with what's-his-face, anyway, haven't you?" The fridge closed. Liza spoke a little louder. "Hey, Ace? Do you have earbuds in or something?"

Her eyes stretched wider, rounder as they met Dayton standing in the mouth of the hallway. She had every right to be shocked. A man she could hardly call an acquaintance was inside her apartment. But as he studied those eyes, golden brown like whiskey, he saw a weak glint of fear.

Hand flying to her chest, Liza exhaled.

"You scared me." When he made no apology, she glanced past him. "Is Kenna here?"

"No. She's out of town."

The spark of fear roared to embers as her brows drew together and an awkward pause hung between them.

"Still? I thought you two traveled together."

Dayton faked a smile, one that sent a searing ache through his cheeks. "We did. She's newly out of town."

"If she's out of town," she took a half step back, "how'd you get in here?"

Panic engulfed him, smothering him like a weighted blanket with each passing breath. A recently awakened impulsivity burned beneath his palms. Blood boiling, veins buzzing. Had Kenna told her roommate that he was involved in a homicide investigation before jumping on a bus to Los Angeles? Responding evenly demanded every ounce of his will.

"She made me a copy of her key."

Liza pinned her arms across her stomach. "Look, our super doesn't allow copies and after what Kenna told me I seriously doubt she'd bend the rule and have one made for you."

"What did she say?"

"The abridged version? She's terrified of you."

Dayton almost laughed. He didn't think Kenna was terrified of him. She was terrified of what she didn't understand. All that he'd refused to help her understand.

Liza's commanding voice broke his reverie.

"I don't know how you weaseled your way in here, but you need to make yourself scarce before I call the police."

24

AUDREY

*T*he sun blazed in the blue sky, warming the people milling about Westwood. It was the kind of weather that would've been categorized as unseasonable for late fall in Oregon. Kenna lingered by the main entrance of the UCLA campus. Audrey had agreed to meet under the condition that it was somewhere public.

From the sidewalk, she recoiled at the traffic, the stench of exhaust, the near constant fragments of passing conversation. In all her life, she'd never set foot in a city as large and imposing as Los Angeles. She tried to ease her trepidation by booking a hotel a couple of blocks from campus.

A tall, curvaceous woman with the familiar pixie cut rounded the corner. Kenna formed a peace sign which she signed in return; their agreed upon signal to identify one another.

Audrey appeared tired but it didn't lessen her beauty. Faint freckles speckled her nose and cheeks. Fine wrinkles radiated from the outer corners of her eyes, a testament to someone who'd spent their life laughing, smiling. It was hard to believe she may have done any of it with a man as austere as Dayton.

"You're younger than I expected." Audrey shook her head slightly. "Let's walk."

Kenna fell into step beside her. A man being pulled on a skateboard by an eager golden retriever sailed past them. Trees sprouted from man-made pockets of dirt in the sidewalk; mother nature fighting for each and every breath amid the cracked asphalt and L.A. smog. That sense of suffocation was all around. No wonder Dayton had felt at home there.

"I guess I don't understand why you came all the way down here to talk to me."

She couldn't fault Audrey for highlighting the absurdity of the situation. Traveling almost a thousand miles to interrogate someone else's past hookup didn't fall into the category of socially acceptable behavior.

"I needed to get out of town anyway. And I was hoping you might be able to give me some answers."

"Answers?" She drew out the word.

Her voice had a raspy, seductive quality and it was easy to see why Dayton had once been enamored with her.

"He told me that you were a one-night stand." Kenna didn't speak his name. There was no need to. "But recently, his sister made a vague comment that led me to believe there's more to the story." She produced a listless sigh. "In my experience, he doesn't do well with confrontation, so I thought I'd try my luck and reach out to you."

"You must really mean something to him if he didn't want you to know about me." Her sunny features went stoney but she brightened in an instant upon spotting a nearby storefront with a red awning. "Do you like cookies?"

Kenna eyed the bakery. "Who doesn't?"

Pulling on the door of the shop, she turned to her and whispered conspiratorially, "Sugar will soften the blow."

The decadent smell, along with Audrey's warning, nearly knocked her off her feet. A sinful mixture of butter, sugar, chocolate, and nuts. Every variety of cookie one could imagine and then some filled a wide glass case. Off to the side, there was a smaller selection of ice creams.

Audrey handled the ordering. Two chocolate chip mint sandwiches, whatever that was, and two waters. Kenna pleaded to cover the cost, as Audrey was doing her a favor in agreeing to the meeting, but she declined the offer.

They settled into a metal table and chairs along the street, confections in tow. Kenna stared at the contents of her paper bowl. Cookies served as the bread in the apparent sandwich and the ice cream as the filling. Rather than make a fool of herself by asking Audrey what it was, she thanked her and took a tentative bite.

It was the purest act of hedonism she'd yet experienced. The gooey chocolate of the warm cookie, the chill of the creamy mint ice cream.

"Wow."

"Lenny's is the best around," she conceded. "He and I used to come here a lot, actually. He'd order oatmeal raisin with pistachio."

"That's vile."

Audrey fought off a smile but was ultimately unsuccessful. And in her failure to suppress it, Kenna lumped her in with all of the other women with whom she'd spoken.

She envied them, in a way.

What memories of her time with Dayton did she have to look back on with any degree of fondness? It occurred to her then, perhaps for the first time, that she was destined to fill a much different role in his life.

One that boasted a higher degree of permanence.

Eating her dessert and staring across the table at yet another woman Dayton had wronged, she wasn't entirely sure she wanted to fill that role.

"Regular ice cream outings sounds more serious than a one-night stand." It sounded juvenile to her own ears but Kenna wasn't sure how to broach the conversation. She fiddled with her St. Rose bracelet, suddenly unsure of herself.

"We were engaged, briefly."

Her stomach bottomed out and she was featherlight, gutted of everything—so why did she feel so heavy? Leaden.

No man nor natural disaster could've evicted her from the chair. Nausea swelled within her, that bubbling elixir, as she came to terms with the fact that she was looking at the woman who was meant to have been Dayton's wife.

Even in her head, it was ludicrous to juxtapose the marital title with his name. He was unfit for marriage.

"You were together for ..." She let the question hang, unfinished. A dark part of her didn't want an answer.

Audrey's gaze fell to the tabletop.

"Two years. I'd like to think we wouldn't have lasted as long if I'd caught on to his behavior. He was always good at hiding his habit." She covered her mouth. There it was. The first sign of her composure wavering. "Watch out for that. You think you know him and then ..."

His habit of photographing sleeping women in their underwear, she wanted to mockingly ask. But she was there to collect rather than reveal information.

Besides, it was clear what Audrey had meant.

Carmen had no trouble disclosing her brother's penchant for infidelity, and from what Kenna had gathered of his sexual habits, he more than likely hadn't had many relationships.

"He cheated on you." Her intonation made it a statement, not a question.

"Has it happened to you too?"

She didn't think Audrey would consent to meeting a total stranger so she had introduced herself as Dayton's girlfriend during their social media exchange and, while it was a departure from the truth, she thought for the purpose of extracting information it was best to adopt a label.

"No, but I wouldn't put it past him."

"A healthy dose of suspicion is good in any relationship. My mom always said that, after I started dating, anyway." Smiling wistfully, she wrapped her arms over her chest, as if shielding herself from more unpleasant memories. "I didn't suspect a thing. No red flags. He was so nice, so charming."

Regrettable nostalgia bathed Audrey's sun-kissed face, giving her the likeness of one of those women in true crime documentaries who carried on a functional relationship with someone who turned out to be a sociopath.

Those women were victims, too, not of the crime but of the compartmentalization.

Audrey insisted that she come to her condo in Silver Lake, assuring her that they could carry on their conversation more comfortably there. Kenna took this as a good sign. In the span of their outing, Audrey must have determined she wasn't a threat and she was counting on that trust. She'd cup it in her palm like a vulnerable seed, shielding it from storms until it grew to its full potential.

She felt out of place in Audrey's swank quarters. Kenna barely afforded her half of the rent and utilities each month in her shared apartment riddled with threadbare furniture scavenged from yard sales.

"You have a lovely home."

Audrey gestured for her to sit on the couch. "Thanks. My boyfriend and I bought it last year."

She joined Kenna on the couch but left a cushion of space between them. A small sense of peace crept over her. It was comforting to know that she had moved on and an even greater comfort that she appeared to lead a normal life. A working professional, a homeowner, in a relationship; but Kenna had spoken to enough of Dayton's ex-lovers to know not to take Audrey Dresden's life at face value.

Something was fractured within Audrey. A missing piece. It was a commonality among them all, a hollowed-out part of their soul fated to eternal vacancy.

Audrey rummaged around beneath the lid of a square piece of furniture. It was quilted and studded with buttons and seemed to serve as a shared ottoman for the couches, though it occupied the usual space of a coffee table. Finally, she retrieved an album, setting it in Kenna's lap.

"Josh hates that I keep this around." She shrugged, her face a portrait of solemnity. "I can't bring myself to get rid of it."

Kenna shot her a wary glance. She ran her fingers over the plain, baby pink vinyl before cracking it open. The images on the first page twisted her insides and the sensation intensified as she flipped through, each page filled with Polaroids of Audrey and Dayton. Shock and jealousy competed for her attention as she slowed her pace and studied the old memories. Her jealousy turned to resentment upon noting the absence of shots where Audrey was half-clothed and asleep.

No, she was awake in every image, smiling and smitten because, for a moment, she had belonged to him.

Their love had been in the light.

Kenna and Dayton's was all scandal and shadows.

She quashed her envy long enough to form a sentence. "I know these are just pictures, but it looks like you two were really in love."

"I loved Dayton." It was the first time she'd heard her say his name. "For a long time, he had me convinced he loved me too."

"Audrey." She employed the gentle tone she'd always used to comfort her sisters. "What happened?"

Her focus fell to the rug. "I told you. He cheated."

"But how did it happen? How did you find out?"

Painstakingly slowly, Audrey turned her head and she stared into her eyes for what seemed like hours but was surely seconds and, as they beheld one another, Kenna grew frightful that the woman beside her had changed her mind. That she had gotten on the Greyhound, something she never thought she'd do again, all in vain.

Soon, the rhythm of Audrey's voice filled the room and something greater than relief washed over her.

"A little after we got engaged, one of my sorority sisters took me aside and admitted she'd slept with Dayton while he and I were together. She was apologetic, tears in her eyes, but I wasn't upset with her because I knew he had this tremendous power to convince a woman she wanted something when in fact she wanted no part of it." Grimness furled her lips. "When Dayton proposed, I looked at the ring in its little cushioned box and I thought, this is moving too fast. I've met his family but he hasn't met mine. I want to stay in the area after college. What if he wants to go out of state after med school? After residency? I looked at that diamond and I knew if I accepted it, I ran the risk of minimizing my career, but I looked into his eyes and it was his face, so open and earnest, that coaxed out my 'yes' because I was afraid of losing his love far more than having my professional life take a backseat to his."

A frightening intensity backlit Audrey's gaze and Kenna redirected her attention to the album, though the endless shots of Dayton's cheerful face didn't provide much relief. She thought of the man she knew and how seldom that same smile surfaced, but didn't allow herself to feel the ensuing pity. Not while she was in the company of another casualty of his love. She recalled what Carmen had said in reference to her brother's habitual cheating. More than once. Multiple women.

But was Audrey privy to the scope of his disloyalty?

"So, he transgressed once with—what did you say her name was?" Her voice sounded detached even to her own ears. A lawyer doing whatever necessary to ensure her client got off.

"Sara. I didn't confront him right away. I don't know why. I guess I was in a post-engagement bubble, thought the universe owed me that moment of ephemeral bliss before reality turned up to remind me that things aren't always so perfect. After Sara came forward, our den mother called a house meeting. She said a couple of girls had come to her, distressed. Those two girls came forward at the meeting and admitted to me, in front of everyone—" Tears glassed in Audrey's eyes. A stiffness settled over her jaw. "That they'd slept with him too."

"It happened with three girls?"

"I wish. They stood up and came clean," she spat the word and made it dirty, "and then my friend Desiree locked eyes with me from across the room and *she* stood up. I was so sick to my stomach. After that, it was like the room exploded. Once our den mother got everyone settled, we went about the admissions in a more cordial manner, like some fucked up trial. I listened to women I thought were close friends admit to sleeping with Dayton. Newer pledges, too, girls I hardly knew. There were 11."

Kenna remembered how numb she had felt glimpsing the Polaroids on his bedroom floor, not necessarily shocked at the discovery of more women but the weight of it.

To understand, without question, that many others had come before her. That she stood among the used.

"You must've confronted him after a scene like that."

"It was ugly. Heartbreaking, to say the least. You've probably figured out by now he's not the kind of guy who takes no for an answer."

A heavy feeling settled in the pit of her stomach. "What do you mean?"

"Once we'd broken up, he broke into the sorority one night, and I mean actual breaking and entering. He was ranting, raving. It's like he was a different person all of a sudden. I tried to run for the stairs so I could get my phone and dial 911 but he grabbed me, wouldn't let go. Pretty much everyone in the house was awake by that point and someone called the police because before I knew it Dayton was in handcuffs and I was at the foot of the staircase, in complete hysterics. Crying, screaming."

"He went to jail?" Her prior knowledge of the arrest made it easier to keep her composure.

"If he did, he didn't stay long. A few days later, one of our mutual friends told me he was hospitalized. I didn't ask for details. I didn't care. Do you know what I said? *Good.* What kind of person says that when they hear news like that?"

Despite their engagement, it seemed she was oblivious to his heart condition. Had he not been hospitalized after the incident in the woods, Kenna wondered if she would have known about it herself.

"Someone who's been hurt." She started to shake her head but stopped short. "Audrey, I am so sorry he did this to you. I can't even imagine what that must have been like." Her thumb ran along the album's spine. "Why do you keep this?"

Audrey lowered her voice, afraid of her own speech.

"I love Josh, I do, but true love is once in a lifetime and mine ended with my ex-fiancé in handcuffs and his bruises on my wrists."

Fear chilled Kenna. The hair rose on her forearms. Though she had hostility toward her love for Dayton, she knew her feelings were just that.

Once in a lifetime.

Upon returning to Branch Spring, she went straight to Fairbrook. The version of Dayton who answered the door looked as if he'd been to Hell and back. An uncharacteristic pallor painted his skin. The same clothes hung on his broad frame as when she'd left days earlier.

He didn't question where she'd gone. Rather, he seemed

grateful for her presence on his doormat. She was thankful, of course, for his silent acceptance.

Hurt and longing swirled in his black irises.

She covered his mouth with an assurance that was gentle but forged. He drew Kenna into his arms and she surrendered fully to the belly of the beast, forgetting her time with Audrey, forgetting the troubling love she carried for him.

Perhaps that was the other women's secret.

Burying everything until they were, inevitably, forced to feel.

January

25

ANOTHER ROUND

Kenna

Kenna sat behind the reception desk, staring out into the empty waiting room. Not one patient had walked through the doors since her shift started three hours earlier.

The landline rested in its cradle, silent.

She had not seen Dayton upon her arrival. He had been holed up in his office the entire afternoon. Door locked. Not that she minded their lack of interaction.

It gave her a break from pretending she didn't know as much as she did; something she should have mastered given all the time they spent together but of which she felt less capable with each passing day.

So many weeks had passed and the conversation with Audrey haunted her as if she'd been the one who lived through it. Her heart had grown cold and black and yet some buried part of it beat for Dayton.

There were three possible versions of her future. She'd move on but carry the collateral for life, like Audrey. She'd beat the odds and stay with him.

Or she'd disappear like Lacey Greene.

Kenna had no intention of welcoming the third option as her fate. When she returned from Los Angeles, she mulled over revisiting her notes and files for the umpteenth time but she was jaded. Exhausted. She had hit a dead end with the Polaroids a long time ago. He denied that the alphabetization bore any significance—not that she believed him. They were all former patients but it seemed like that was where the connection began and ended.

For curiosity's sake, she had asked Audrey to recall as many of the women's names as she could but they were all over the board. No order like the girls in the box.

Down the hall, a door clicked, followed by the clacking of dress shoes.

"It's dead in here," she said.

Dayton's eyes drifted toward her in passing as he approached the set of metal blinds in the corner of the waiting area. "I wonder why that is."

He twisted the wand, cloaking him in shadows, and her pulse sped up, as if a hummingbird were trapped in her throat. He slunk to the next set and closed them, then opened the front door long enough to flip the sign to 'closed' before shutting it once more, locking it, and pocketing the key.

Kenna swallowed, snatching her bag off the floor, on her feet faster than she could blink. "I can take a hint. I'll head out."

The corner of his mouth twitched as he shut the second to last set of blinds. "You're not going anywhere. Sit."

Slowly, she lowered herself back into the chair. Her bag's strap slid off her shoulder and it dropped to the ground.

He closed the final set and a veil of darkness fell over the room. She could only identify his outline but that was menacing enough as he stalked toward her.

His arms locked around her middle and she stayed stiff as a

corpse until he lifted her onto the reception desk. Stillness ruled the dark. His steady breathing. Her thundering heart.

"We had a full afternoon."

The same sense of dread as when she'd found the box overtook her. But Kenna wasn't new to feeling threatened in his presence. "Had?"

"I called and rescheduled their appointments."

"Why?"

One-word responses weren't her style but she was doing all she could to maintain a calm exterior. Meanwhile, a bevy of nails scraped at her skin.

He took a step closer, fingers ghosting across her cheek. "I thought we could benefit from some alone time."

"We see each other almost every day."

"The girl I've been seeing may as well be a lobotomy victim. Where's your beautiful mind run off to?"

His palms slid up her thighs and she cursed herself for wearing a dress. Every ounce of breath fled Kenna's lungs as his thumbs dug into her flesh and she thought, once again, of those phantom nails tearing through her muscles and carving into her bones.

"Dayton." She meant to stop him but it came out more suggestive than she'd intended.

Her stinging skin called out to some hidden part of herself. It was as if she'd been asleep all her life, waiting to be awoken by his burning, bruising touch.

She knew it was wrong to take pleasure in their intimacy. She shouldn't have coveted him, worked for him, spoken to him. Light once shone from the hole where she'd tumbled but now there was only darkness. Escaping was no longer a possibility. Survival, essential.

For she was doomed to love him.

"I know you've been faking it lately, lamb." A chill coiled around her spine as Dayton dragged his lips along her neck, up to her ear, whispering, "Disingenuous is a word I never would've associated with you when you stepped into my office last winter."

"A lot's changed since then. I've changed."

"Yet you remain hopelessly naive."

"What's that supposed to mean?"

He caught her earlobe between his teeth and pulled it before migrating to her neck once more. Kenna shut her eyes in an attempt to muster some resolve but all hope was lost as his thumb slowly traced an imaginary seam along the center of her underwear before he backtracked and produced tiny, teasing circles. "You're looking so hard, you're blinded by what's right in front of you. Things are much more simple than you'd like to believe." His words were flames licking her neck as his thumb applied greater pressure and she breathed in steadily through her nose, fighting to remain clearheaded while ignoring the heat raging low in her abdomen, like liquid mercury. "Oh, but you grew up sheltered and as a result, you are relentlessly paranoid. Who is this man? What has he done with these poor women? That's something I love about you. You have to assign such meaning to everything."

A blinding white pain shot through Kenna as his teeth sank into her neck with jarring force. The sound that fled from her lips equally indicated her arousal and shock. Whatever will she once possessed to escape was extracted as Dayton's teeth remained connected to her, sucking the delicate skin.

"Stop."

Her whisper was static, lost amid their breathing, and he did not oblige the request. His greedy mouth migrated to an unmarked patch of skin and his thick fingers tore at her underwear.

"I said *stop*." She repeated with greater force. Her hand shot out and, startled by her own strength, she seized his wrist. "Maybe you've played games with everyone else but that's not going to work with me."

Dayton smiled but it didn't reach his eyes. They remained pitch black. No glimmer of light.

"No, darling. I'm finished with games. You're the fucking prize."

Perhaps she should've been flattered but her first instinct was to leave the office. She loved him, she did, but she did so quietly. On her own terms. He did not yet know she reciprocated those feelings and feared surrendering the knowledge of that love to him. The admission would become another weapon in his arsenal.

She managed a level tone despite the elixir of emotions rearing to alter it. "I'm going home. Pay me for the rest of the afternoon or don't. I don't care."

Dayton

The Rusted Monkey was busier than usual. Louder. People were crammed into the galley-style establishment, either ignorant or uncaring that they had a fire code.

Too many yet somehow not enough 'excuse me's and 'I'm sorry's were tossed around as patrons continuously bumped into Nathan and Dayton at the bar. The place had become a macabre tourist attraction since Lacey's strangled corpse was found in the dumpster. There was nowhere to go to get away from the girl's death. It had left a permanent mark on the town.

And he was at the decaying center of it all, evidenced by Detective Reynolds stationed at the opposite end of the bar.

His lingering presence in their sleepy town raised a number of red flags. The investigation was ongoing but their efforts had shifted toward locating and extraditing Shane Sanders. So why was Reynolds hanging around when all of his law enforcement cronies were exhausting every possible resource in what was quickly turning into a national manhunt?

No one else would've known he was a detective. He was just an average guy, having a drink. He could have held any number of jobs with his suits and sleek vehicle. But Dayton knew there was a gun holstered across the back of his dress shirt, a badge within his pocket, and a searing hatred behind his steely gaze.

Reynolds nodded at him, raising his glass of cheap domestic beer.

Dayton forced himself to look away, redirecting his attention to his friend. Staring at the detective who wanted to see him strung up by his ankles like a slaughtered animal wasn't in his best interest.

Recently, Nathan had his old, electric green frames fitted with new lenses, in the hopes they'd entertain the baby during the many sleepless nights that were in his and Charlaine's not so distant future.

It was hard to take him seriously with all of that neon contorted around his eyes, but it transported him to those early days when he had so openly taken Dayton under his wing. When he was new to the university and had no one. He found himself thinking of that often, although anyone was bound to turn nostalgic when fearing their home may be stormed by the FBI while they slept.

"Who's that guy?" Nathan asked.

"Some asshole," he muttered into his club soda, watching the drink fizz with disdain.

His first attempt to give up alcohol had been shattered when Kenna returned at summer's end. His second, and current, stint of sobriety was threatened on a daily basis ever since he was forced to live in the shadow of a homicide detective.

Nathan glanced between him and the soda. "You aren't drinking. What's up with that?"

Dayton looked his friend, his only friend, in the eye and contemplated telling him what he had kept hidden their entire relationship. Coming out and saying it seemed too dangerous. Too real. That descriptor was beginning to fit too many things in his life.

"I'm dying, Nathaniel."

"That's pretty dramatic. You do seem down, lately, though." He drained the rest of his bottle and Dayton watched in envy as the last of the hops disappeared. "You need to come back to St. James, that's what you need to do. Kenna shows up to Mass every week without fail, and you? You treat God like a tramp on a street corner. You go into that box and take an hour of their time and then you go back to pretending neither of them exist."

"Church is the last place I need to be."

"Just trying to help." Nathan held up his hands but swiftly transitioned to pulling something out of his pocket. "Hey, take a look at this." He unfolded a piece of paper. A sonogram. "It's a boy."

"That's really great, man. Congratulations."

The well wishes were acid on his tongue.

He looked at the grainy photo, that new life, and it reminded him of what he could never have. Not that Kenna was in a position to consider having a family with him, even if they were able. They were stuck in a cycle of emotionless sex and dead-end conversations; not to mention the fact that she had yet to reciprocate his love. He placed the blame solely on Audrey. Before Kenna had left for California, they were in a reasonably good place, building brick by brick toward a healthy relationship. She may have been disinclined to put that label on it but he'd long ago come to the consensus that she didn't know what was good for her.

Dayton threw back the last of his drink and slid the empty glass toward the inside of the counter. He rose unceremoniously from the stool. "I have to piss."

"You want me to order another round?"

"Hilarious, Nate."

He all but shoved his way through the crowd but found no solace in the men's room. Footsteps trailed behind him, crashing his party of one. The owner of the noisy shoes claimed the neighboring urinal and he was far from surprised upon uncovering his identity. A mix of hate and irritation slithered in to fill the space between them.

Detective Reynolds side-eyed him, violating an unspoken rule of public restroom etiquette. "Here for trivia?"

"Michael keeps canceling recently. He thinks it isn't practical to play with all of the extra foot traffic from these true crime junkies. I come every week in spite of it."

What possessed him to speak to Reynolds at all, he did not know. Dayton was agitated beyond belief, and judging by the tone he had taken with the detective, he was doing a piss-poor job of hiding it. The decorative neon wall signs blinked mischievously, as if they were his brain, shutting down, and the room felt like it was losing square footage by the second. Squeezing his insides, thieving the oxygen.

His only thought was getting out of there.

He zipped up and moved to the sink where he scrubbed his hands hard enough to remove a layer of skin.

"So, your routine hasn't changed, even after the murder. You're a creature of habit."

Their eyes met in the mirror and it extinguished any of the vertigo he'd felt moments earlier. "And a victim of circumstance."

Reynolds averted his gaze. The desired result. He approached to wash his hands but Dayton acted as a barrier between him and the industrial basin.

"If you're going to arrest me for something, arrest me. Or maybe you can't and that's why you're following me around, hoping I'll mess up. You have no real evidence against me. Sanders' face is the one plastered all over the news night after night, not mine, and I refuse to fall for your intimidation tactics."

His face was neutral. Tone even.

"We'll see about that, doctor."

Dayton's vertigo came creeping back, tingeing every one of his senses, but he managed to text Kenna as he re-emerged in the bar area. *I need to see you. Tonight.*

No reply came.

February

26

ACCESSORY

Kenna

$\mathcal{K}$enna climbed the stairs in Duniway Hall. Her eyes stayed glued on her boots.

There was no avoiding the snide remarks as she passed other students but she was thankful that she didn't catch their nasty, accompanying expressions. She reached the second-floor landing and headed for Research Methods I, heart beating wildly in her chest, cheeks flushed.

Her involvement with Dayton was the scandal of the century at Ponderosa. Word of their affair had survived more than two semesters. Summer break. Fall break. Winter break.

The students didn't forget.

She had no right to be livid. The rumors were true. Perhaps she was more outraged that everyone on campus knew about her sex life. That she'd done the deed with the dark doctor.

Even her professors regarded her with outright disdain. Weren't they supposed to take her side, believe she had been taken advantage of and condemn Dayton?

188

Instead, they treated her like a lecherous temptress. She had done this. He was not to blame. Powerless to resist.

Her fingers flew to her neck to relieve the itching skin beneath her scarf. Scarves were not an article of clothing she favored, but she had been all but forced to go out and buy one to disguise her black and blue skin or risk further humiliation.

When she'd examined the dark and mottled mark in the bathroom mirror the previous evening, she feared the skin was broken. She cleaned it with hydrogen peroxide before sinking to the floor, where she cried like an inconsolable child until Liza knocked on the door, politely inquiring about the possibility of a shower.

A hand clamped on her shoulder and she spun around so fast, it took her vision a moment to catch up. Kenna was caught off guard by the guy who stood before her with stiff curls and blue eyes. Seeing him now triggered a cruel but concise montage. The bar, the drinks, the warnings, the good times in between. But she'd alienated herself from all of that.

From them.

"Will."

"It's been a while. Kind of weird our schedules haven't overlapped since grad school started, considering we're in the same program."

"Yeah, it is weird."

She was in no mood to chat, especially not with someone who witnessed her emerging romance with Dayton firsthand.

"You alright? You look exhausted."

Despite the slow nod she managed, Kenna failed to convince even herself. She knew her fatigue betrayed that assurance. Balancing all of her obligations and dealing with the stress of the investigation was running her into the ground. She'd never worn concealer in all her life until a few weeks ago, when the rings beneath her eyes had grown too dark to cover with powder.

They moved at a snail's pace toward the east hallway; she presumed Will's class was also housed there. His brows pulled together but his gaze was focused ahead, as if he were afraid to look at Kenna.

One look at the temptress, purveyor of academic ruin, might sully one's reputation.

"Did you get an off-campus job? Not to be nosy. It's just, I haven't seen you around the library."

"I work at Dayton's practice, over in East Haven."

"Dayton?"

It wasn't until she detected the questioning note in his voice that she registered the mistake. She quickly amended, "Dr. Merino."

"Oh."

That one syllable was so soft, so telling. She interpreted it as his censored version of 'that explains a lot.'

"Hey, there's a party in the woods tomorrow off 99, a few miles past Roth's. Bonfire. Beer. You should come. No offense, but you really look like you could use a night out."

Refusal rose in her throat like bile but she swallowed it down. Will was right. She was overdue for an evening of conformity.

"I'll be there."

Her last class let out at 11:15 and she headed straight for the parking lot, as per her usual routine. The noon shift at the practice didn't leave much time for dallying but Kenna preferred her days that way. Busy, structured.

Graduate school and her affair with Dayton combined forces and effectively extinguished her social life. She realized, with a sad sort of clarity, that she hadn't exactly missed the trivia outings or occasional parties. So, why had she agreed to the bonfire? To appease Will Morris? Certainly not.

Either way, the damage was done. She had already accepted the invitation. If she backed out, she ran the risk of starting a rumor that *Dr. Merino* was keeping her on a tight leash.

Something sank in her stomach as she approached the station wagon. What if Will had invited her for entertainment value? Her chest flared with rage only long enough to resolve that a plus-one was in order, welcome or otherwise.

The tip of the key had barely grazed the lock when a high-pitched whistle caught her attention.

Kenna spotted Detective Reynolds standing a few cars down and the sinking sensation intensified, as if everything inside of her fell away. Lost forever.

"Miss O'Callaghan." He crooked a skinny finger, beckoning her over to his SUV.

Walking toward him, her heart thrummed with the delayed enthusiasm of a well-worn instrument and when they stood within several feet of each other, she offered no greeting.

Reynolds surveyed the vicinity before yanking open the passenger door. "Get in."

"Excuse me?"

"Get in the car. We're going on a field trip."

She obeyed, more worried about being spotted by students than whatever the detective had in store.

Their destination, as it turned out, was a diner rather than the precinct. Kenna relaxed a bit once they were surrounded by other people and the smell of comfort food.

They were escorted to their table and, once she caught sight of the formica, she remembered drinking coffee on that rainy after-noon with Brandi as they awaited the arrival of her sister, Erin. The memory seemed as if it happened yesterday yet was far, far removed. Now, she found herself in the company of a detective. A scarf looped around her neck, hiding bruises from view à la Lacey Greene the day she'd burst into Dayton's office.

It was a marvel, really, how much a year could change things.

Reynolds mirrored the mannerisms of any other patron. He

drank his black coffee while scanning the menu, replacing the mug and muttering, "Tastes like shit."

A deep-set wrinkle framed either side of his mouth and she suspected the premature aging was a result of duress, not felicity. There was something about the sharpness of his facial features, all lines and angles, that Kenna found attractive. The gold ring on his finger made her feel impish for thinking so.

The waitress came around to take their order and Kenna declined Reynolds' offer for a bite to eat. She was content to sip her water, knowing that any ounce of food she tried to keep down would've encouraged her increasing need to vomit.

"Why didn't you bring me to the station?"

She never would have dared to ask the question pre-Dayton. During the time she had known him, she'd gradually metamorphosed into a brazen young woman whose light voice had adopted a dangerous edge. A razor blade cutting through silk. It wasn't an entirely new version of herself.

Instead, it was a part she kept hidden, called upon as a last defense when she felt like the whole world was collapsing around her. She'd experienced that feeling on two occasions.

Fleeing the farm to leave on a Greyhound bus in the middle of the night and sitting across from Detective Reynolds in a seedy diner.

"Let's just say I've overstayed my welcome."

His spoon clanked against the walls of the mug as he stirred in sugar substitute and the loud, ensuing noise made Kenna shift atop the vinyl-upholstered bench.

"Look, my lieutenant's about ready to hang me over zeroing in on the search for Sanders so we can extradite him. We have something pretty damning on Merino, but the LT doesn't think it's enough to carry the court case on its own and we're working with a body and dump site that are clean as a whistle. That being said, he wouldn't approve of me using resources to question you in an official capacity. So here we are. I just want to ask you a few harmless questions, see if it gets me anywhere."

"No one believes you?"

He held her gaze a moment too long, perhaps cogitating in amusement over her words, before whipping a tiny notebook and pen out of his pocket. "You know what they say, it's always the husband. Or in this case, the boyfriend."

"Can I ask you one thing first?"

"Fair enough."

"What does your wife think about all of this? What you do for a living, I mean? Is she ever … afraid?"

"I wouldn't know. She died nine years ago. But I have her to thank for my career. Identifying your wife's body after she's been murdered in cold blood is enough to make any sane man take on the badge."

"I had no idea. I am so terribly—"

"Save it. I've heard it all."

He asked to see her license so he could record it as part of his record for the case and she wordlessly complied. A stack of pancakes arrived at the table. Reynolds held a fork in one hand and his pen in the other. Kenna was disastrously unprepared for whatever lay ahead, but if Dayton had taught her anything it was to think on her feet.

After a couple of bites, he broke into the questioning. "Would you describe your boyfriend as someone who's meticulous?"

"He isn't my boyfriend."

"He seems to think otherwise. Answer the question."

"Yes, he's meticulous."

"You spend the night at his place pretty often. Good sex life?"

"I don't see how that's relevant or even appropriate here, detective."

"Let me rephrase that. Does he cause physical harm to you while you're in bed? Biting? Choking? Restraints? Anything like that?"

Phantom sensations assailed her body. Dayton's teeth sinking into her skin. His bruising fingers branding her flesh.

Physical harm. Is that how she would've described it?

"No, nothing like that."

"You know how she died?"

She shook her head.

"Asphyxiation." He said this while examining her neck. "Nice scarf." Reynolds looked at her through his lashes, a wolf on the prowl, and it was that subtle incline of his head that transformed him from good cop to bad cop. "You know what an accessory is, Miss O'Callaghan? And I don't mean that pretty little thing tied around your neck. If you conceal a crime, you're guilty under perjury of the law."

"I have a firm grasp on the law, sir."

"Your fake driver's license says otherwise."

Her protests died on her tongue.

"Don't worry, I'm not going to book you. I'm balls deep in this investigation. I don't have time for misdemeanors." He took another sip of coffee, reviewing lines in his notebook. "You were there the day I showed up with the search warrant. Did he ever tell you what led to that?"

Stuffing the final sopping bite of pancakes into his mouth, he chewed and smiled like whatever he was about to say was the funniest thing in the world. He spoke while motioning with his fork. "Dayton Merino was the last known person to see Lacey Greene alive. And if I find out that you're helping this sick fuck, covering up for him in any way, you better believe I plan to risk my career to nail you both."

With that, he slapped a stack of bills on the table and walked away, leaving Kenna pulling on her scarf, throat burning.

2 7

BONFIRE

Kenna

$\mathcal{N}$ ight had fallen over the trees. Stars dotted the sky like feral diamonds and a blaze of orange light glowed off in the distance, illuminating the trunks of the pines.

Kenna didn't know what possessed her to invite Dayton to the bonfire but she quietly regretted the bold choice as he parked amid the sea of cars.

He was mute in the driver's seat. They had scarcely exchanged a handful of words since he'd picked her up from the apartment complex. She reasoned the quiet animosity was a direct result of missing her shift at the practice the prior afternoon. He hadn't the faintest idea where she had been, and while she feared his reaction to the news, the thought of what he may have done if she opted not to tell him terrified her far more.

Staring out the windshield, he asked, "Where the hell were you yesterday?"

She didn't look at him, not fully. Peripheral glances. "I lied to Reynolds."

The name-drop granted her his full attention.

"You lied to a detective? To an officer of the law? When did—" He cut himself off, eyes darkening as realization dawned. "You were with him yesterday."

Kenna had never seen him adopt such a furious look and her every impulse begged her to yank the door handle, barrel out of the car and run into the woods. She'd run until her feet bled and her insides exploded.

Her arms were limp. She didn't reach for the handle.

This wasn't last year.

She had no intention of hopping on her bicycle and riding away from his endless parade of horrors, even if it meant, by some wretched twist of fate, that she'd become one of them.

"Dayton, they got a warrant and turned your house upside down. How many times has Reynolds questioned you? And now, he's questioned me. They're looking at you hard for this. If there's anything you're not telling me—"

"*Enough.*"

The harsh command dissuaded her monologue from going any further. What Reynolds had revealed to her about Lacey stayed secret. Why should she reveal what he wasn't willing to tell?

His low voice cut the silence. "If you're having second thoughts, I can go."

Her hand covered his, though she didn't hold it nor squeeze it. It lay limp over his own in half-hearted assurance.

"I want you to stay."

She willed herself to believe the statement that served as a bandage over their heated exchange.

Truthfully, Kenna had invited him because she thought if other students saw them together, the sighting would finally kill the buzz on campus about their romance.

He leaned across the console and pressed a single kiss to her lips, eyes roaming her face when he pulled back. "You're stunning tonight, Miss O'Callaghan. I recommend you stay by my side, lest a lecherous boy claim you for himself."

She laughed. The sound was weak, punctuated by too much breath, but a laugh nonetheless.

It was a moment she wished would never end.

Alone together in his car as a party raged around them. Dayton making her laugh. Something bubbled within her that had been absent for so long. Happiness.

How was it possible to feel even that fleeting joy amid the grim landscape in which their relationship existed?

Those bubbles popped as she shut the car door and met Dayton in front of the hood. Kenna looked at him and saw the blight—all of the reasons her happiness was inappropriate—but she also saw an invasive vine.

Love blossoming in the face of destruction.

They walked toward the orange glow and the acrid stench of smoke intensified. Her nerves grew tenfold with every step and her chest hitched as he looped an arm around her waist. He had never held her in that manner and it was decidedly possessive in spite of its simplicity. She felt like the rebel of the century. Her mentor turned lover turned boss slash potential murder suspect on her arm.

It was official. She was going to Hell.

They drew closer to the light, the music. *Possum Kingdom* blared in all of its grunge glory from an unidentified speaker. In Branch Spring, bands like Toadies and Nirvana got as much airplay as whoever was topping the charts and people wore too many flannels and thought they were way cooler than anyone else. Didn't anyone tell them they were 220 miles southwest of Seattle?

With Dayton's arm still locked around her waist, they emerged in the clearing. The crowd was relatively small for a college party, less than 100 people. Everyone in attendance was a grad student and Will had informed her that it was by personal invite only.

He hadn't said anything about a plus-one.

Every head turned and eyed them as though they were disgraced royalty and so they didn't kneel at their feet, only stared on in disbelief.

Kenna had expected whispers and the inevitable stares but as they held the attention of the entire crowd she wondered, for the second time, if bringing Dayton had been a mistake.

"Let's get a beer and give them a chance to catch their breath," he whispered, guiding her by the arm toward a large, open cooler.

He grabbed two bottles, twisted off the caps with his bare hands, and offered her one. The cheap hops fell flat on her tongue and she had no real interest in finishing the drink, but she kept it in her hand for the sake of blending in. Kenna's grip tightened on the longneck as a chill rocked through her. To calm herself, she studied their surroundings.

Rather than one massive bonfire, fires roared in three separate pits. Strands of lights coiled around trees outside of a small cabin. People milled in and out of its screen door, some idling on the porch.

A sharp crack drew her attention back to Dayton. He was opening another beer. How long had she zoned out?

"We could still leave."

"Everyone saw us."

"I thought that's what you wanted."

"It doesn't matter what I want." The words seared her throat.

She wanted the gossip to die. She wanted everything he had done to have been nothing more than an elaborate nightmare. She wanted to wake up in his arms and be reassured that everything was normal.

Yet things were growing more complicated by the day and, though her feelings for him should have waned, they only intensified. She was determined to hold onto him and whatever they had, even if she didn't fully understand why.

"Everyone saw us," she repeated softly.

He opened his mouth as if to speak but someone cut him off prematurely. A familiar voice.

"Kenna," Will called from across the way. Beer in hand, he jogged over to them, features tensing as he registered who was at her side but still sparing Dayton a courteous nod. "Dr. Merino."

He pointed at Will. "Will Morris."

"Impressive memory."

"Hardly. We see each other every week."

"Mind if I steal Kenna for a few minutes?"

"Not at all. As long as you bring her back."

He faltered under Dayton's penetrative stare and Kenna restrained her laughter as she and Will walked off toward the only vacant fire pit. She made the mistake of tossing her hair over her shoulder. Between the moonlight and the flames, there was no hope in hiding the bite marks.

"Whoa. What the hell happened to your neck?" He craned his head to better examine it, hand reaching out.

She stopped him before he made contact. "Don't."

They sank into a pair of worn camper chairs.

"So it is true," he lamented. "Why him? He's a creep."

She didn't bother defending Dayton nor her love for him. It didn't matter what Will thought. Shooting him a pointed look, she changed the subject.

"Do you guys still go to trivia?"

"Every Thursday. You should really come sometime. The team's changed. Brandi moved to Portland. And so there were three. But Liam's girlfriend joins in on occasion. She's a little older than us but she's cool."

"Good to know he's doing well."

"Just so you know, he was torn up when you rejected him. For months."

"I didn't reject him."

"Well, you didn't really give him a chance either." Will raised his brows, as if daring her to challenge him, and then something shifted in his features. His gaze fell to the dirt. "We stopped going for a while, after the whole Lacey thing. Freaked everyone out." He took a long sip from his beer and found the courage to meet her eyes. "We were there when they found her. They stopped trivia but made everyone stay until they'd collected statements. Someone swore there were fingers dangling out of the dumpster. Maybe they were exaggerating, but God, can you imagine? I'm surprised you weren't there that night."

"Why would I have been?"

"You know, since you're sleeping with Dr. Jekyll and Mr. Hyde. But then I guess it figures you weren't there because it's a school hangout. Don't want to feed those rumors. Speaking of, why exactly did you bring him tonight?"

Kenna's blood ran cold. Not even the warmth of the fire thawed her veins. "Dayton was there?"

"Dayton," Will repeated with distaste.

"*Will.*"

"Yeah, he was there, alright? And Professor Scott."

She didn't offer him a goodbye as she sprang out of the chair and headed back to where she'd left Dayton. Will shouted after her above the din of the party but she didn't acknowledge him and his pleas faded into nonexistence as she neared Dayton and the circle of students he stood among.

She stumbled into the group mid-conversation.

"The tightest p—" Dayton stopped talking as one of the guys mimed a neck slicing motion at him, nodding to Kenna.

"... Person-environment fit. Fascinating stuff."

Stopping short of his toes, she spoke through gritted teeth. "We need to talk. Right. Now."

A few guys provided unnecessary commentary.

"The lady doth protest too much, methinks."

"She can protest all she wants with her tight little *person-environment fit.* That shit will brainwash you into putting up with anything."

She buried her rising outrage over whatever distasteful things had been said in her absence and grabbed Dayton by the hand, leading him away from the pack of boys.

He was much too inebriated to refuse her grasp.

As they traveled farther from the party, the noise faded and the fire's glow dimmed. Wandering into the woods with a potential killer wasn't the brightest idea but she knew they were the talk of the party and she'd be damned if anyone overheard their conversation.

Even if it was their last.

Dayton

The pines swayed, everything around him spinning, as she led him through the forest. He had lost track of how many beers he'd consumed—somewhere between two and enough to open up to a group of students about his and Kenna's sex life. And then she had returned from her chat with the Morris boy, understandably upset about what she had either overheard or inferred.

Even in his drunken state, Dayton was confident he could charm her into forgetting the vulgar conversation. But when she led him far enough into the creeping pines, he realized that wasn't the issue.

She stared at him as if she had been fatally betrayed and a deep ache plunged into his chest, spreading to his limbs, fingers, toes.

"You were there that night."

Her tone wasn't accusatory but matter-of-fact. She knew the truth and dared him to refute it.

"I was."

Kenna huffed and looked away, eyes snapping back to him. "All this time and you didn't say anything."

For all her fury, she kept her voice low.

They'd attracted a great deal of attention at the party and

getting caught discussing a crime would have only fast-tracked their ascension in the ranks of Ponderosa infamy.

"I decided it was best not to tell you."

"Why would you even consider keeping something like this from me?"

"Because I knew you'd react like this." His voice rose to its usual volume, which equated to shouting amid their hushed dialogue.

"Like this how? Like an appropriate way to respond? This is insane." Her eyes shut and when they opened they focused on the sky, the treetops. Everywhere but him. "I don't know if you're aware, but in the event of a *murder*, too many coincidences usually equals guilt. Now I know why Reynolds is all over your case."

"You're believing Reynolds' theories now?"

"I've never known what to believe with you, Dayton. I've listened to women divulge terrible things about you and yet I've wound up in your arms. You need to start telling me the truth because …"

She trailed off, swallowing thickly as she leaned against a tree trunk. He drew his body to hers. Tangling a hand in her hair, he forced her to meet his gaze.

"Say it."

"I can't lose you. I can't lose you and most days I hate myself for it but I can't get rid of it. I can't change it."

He had longed to hear Kenna say something to that effect though he hadn't expected it to come in the woods under the veil of night. Joy sobered him and he dropped kisses on her cheeks, her lips. "I was beginning to wonder if I meant anything to you."

She pushed him lightly to break the kisses.

"No more lies. No more secrets."

"Darling, since you came back into my life I've acted only in the interest of protecting what we have."

Taking her into his arms, he cradled her head against his chest and found himself struck by the ugly honesty of his own words.

28
FLOORBOARDS

Dayton

*T*he small, sterile exam room was a five-star accommodation compared to the jail cell he somehow continued to narrowly avoid.

Dayton would just as soon end his own life than spend the rest of his days on the inside, at which point he may as well kiss his precious research project goodbye. Files upon files sitting on his computer, forgotten.

Nine years in the making and nothing to show.

A sharp pain shot through his head, as if someone had taken a chisel to his skull, and he winced in response. He'd prepared to assure the doctor that he was ready to start fresh and kick his old habits yet there he was nursing a hangover.

Dr. Stein entered the room, looking less than amused as he waved around a manila folder. "Bad news."

He plopped onto a rolling stool and its cushion exhaled. Dayton consulted the ceiling before dealing with the balding man who sat before him.

"Just how bad?"

"High blood pressure. You're a healthy person, considering everything you're up against. I'd like your consent for a tox screening."

"That won't be necessary."

"All for the best." He slapped the folder onto the counter. "We both know what I'd find."

"I'm only human."

"Not much longer at the rate you're going." Dr. Stein released a crude laugh. "I've asked you to give up the solo running and I've asked you to ditch the cannabis. You were doing alright with the alcohol until recently. You're a doctor yourself, Dayton, so tell me, what do you do with insubordinate patients?"

When it became clear he wasn't going to respond, the doctor carried on with his spiel. "You know I can't give you beta blockers because of your unique comorbidity, so I'm afraid if you can't follow the lifestyle changes I suggest, I have to release you from my care."

Time slowed. The clock's second hand teetered back and forth, stuck in place, rather than moving forward. And even with a moment to think, he still acted against the premature regret he felt.

Extending a hand, Dayton said, "I suppose we're finished, if that's the case."

Though he admitted it was his own doing, Dayton was miffed at having been officially released. He was the only physician in the area seasoned enough—and, quite frankly, the only one willing—to take on a patient in his condition.

The search for a replacement provider was bound to be extensive and exhausting, and it would involve driving to Portland, perhaps farther, for appointments.

Yes, the process would require a great deal of time and energy, something he possessed little of at present.

A more urgent matter had to be dealt with.

Rows upon rows of diamonds gleamed within the confines of the glass display case. The last time he'd given a woman a ring, it had been thrown at him while he was dragged away in handcuffs. He knew purchasing another was gambling with fate. There was no guarantee his engagement to Kenna wouldn't end the same way.

"Let me know if there's a particular piece you'd like to take a closer look at," said the gray-haired woman behind the counter.

Dayton half-nodded in assent. He had few brain cells available for processing speech. His mind was a million places at once. Reynolds had not made an appearance in a while but he feared he was still observing from afar. Monitoring him.

Or at least that was the scenario he needed to believe if he wanted to survive. Hence the trip to the jewelry store.

He had to be prepared to one-up Reynolds on the off chance something was discovered that put him, rather than Sanders, behind bars for life. At least he'd get proper medical care.

If Kenna were to testify during the Greene trial, it'd be the opening of Pandora's box.

Kenna

Dayton had roped her into spending the night after her heartfelt confession at the bonfire and she'd accepted, not because they had entered some higher level of intimacy, but rather she knew he had a cardiology appointment the following morning.

Meaning, she'd have the entire house to herself.

Kenna had been to his home countless times but she had never been alone in the space, free to roam and peruse without the threat of his watchful gaze.

First, she chose the backyard—somewhere she had seen only through the bedroom windows.

The yard was lush but modest in size. Unfenced. There was a well-manicured garden, not dissimilar to the one at the front of the house, along with some rose bushes and youthful trees. She half expected to find a creepy shed. There was nothing of the kind. Instead, he kept his bare-bones assortment of yard tools and fertilizer beneath a tarp against a corner of the house.

Kneeling by a section of the garden, she was overwhelmed by an array of scents that were anything but floral. She smelled ginger, honey, and coffee grounds. She recalled seeing Dayton slip through the back door carrying a plate piled high with decaf remnants and tea leaves.

Incredible. He even manipulated the soil.

For all Kenna knew, the patch of dirt could've been riddled with the teeth of lovers past.

Why did she continue to leave room for the possibility that he was a killer? He didn't have the best track record for repressing carnal urges with the likes of his former patients and mentees, but that didn't mean his malevolence bent to more violent ends. Even after what Reynolds had revealed. She herself had said coincidences often pointed to guilt, but his guilt in this scenario would bury her.

Spreading her hand in the soil, she was greeted by the cold, wet earth molding around her skin. Kenna welcomed that sensation, letting it calm her and chase away the paranoia.

There was an explanation. Missing pieces, like always.

Once inside, she scrubbed the dirt from under her nails at the kitchen sink. She considered the living room briefly but her footfalls guided her to the bedroom.

The site of her darkest discovery the previous spring.

She lowered herself to the hardwood and looked under the bed even though she knew the box no longer resided there. The empty space perhaps made her more uneasy, not knowing if Dayton had kept it and simply stored it elsewhere or if he'd gotten rid of it altogether.

Her knee brushed the rug at the foot of the bed and she recoiled as flashes of memories came back to her.

Stumbling in and out of the bathroom. Falling to the ground. Feeling as though she'd been drugged. How quickly it all had passed, like the episode was a contrivance of her imagination.

At the edge of the rug, Kenna noticed that one of the floor planks was loose, raised slightly above the others. But as she peeled the rug back, it revealed more loose boards. She'd discovered three by the time she cleared the area.

The longer she stared at them, the faster her heart beat.

She should've replaced the rug, gotten up, and walked away, but she found herself clawing at the floorboards until the planks laid beside her in a haphazard pile and she stared down into the darkened space. DVDs. An entire archive.

Dayton wouldn't be away all morning.

She didn't have long.

An unpleasant odor emanated from the secret compartment and she grimaced while combing through the discs. Each one bore either a weird phrase or a date. All but one, which Kenna retrieved with shaking hands.

Gray October, Sung-Min Park.

She had suspected that Dayton had been the one who'd slashed Liam's tires, and perhaps that he'd also stolen the short film, but now she held the proof.

His appearance outside of Wagner Theatre that cold February night had, in fact, not been a coincidence.

She set the film aside and resumed filing through the discs, but staring at the collection in their cases didn't do her any good. Kenna resolved to watch just one, if only to advance her research. She selected one at random. Its label read, '09.10.18.' For a motion-less moment, she studied his familiar penmanship and wondered if watching it would further tear down her faith in him, faith that had been running on fumes for months and months yet never depleted.

Deep down, she knew nothing she learned or uncovered would eliminate that faith. Not when she was the only thing keeping it alive.

Migrating back to the main area of the house, she settled in at the desk and popped the disc into his laptop.

Her heart hammered as her eyes flicked between the wall clock and the screen. Kenna could only imagine how Dayton would react were he to come home and find her screening his home movies.

It was dark and the camera was shaky but a woman soon came into focus. Her voice was high and had a breathy quality as she repeatedly said 'no' between laughs, holding her palms out in front of the camera to block herself from view. A larger hand reached out and softly batted hers out of the way, revealing the woman from the navel up, and every hair on Kenna's body stood on end as a deeper voice spoke.

"That's better. Now everyone can see your beautiful face."

"Everyone? You promised this was just for us."

"It's a figure of speech, Jazz."

Jazz. The nickname played on a loop through her head as she took note of the distinctive red bra. She was one of the Polaroid girls. Long lashes cast shadows across her face, a reluctant smile blooming as she ran a hand through her straight dark brown hair.

Jasmine.

She sat up, leaning forward, and the angle of the camera fell to the sheets, at which point Kenna ejected the disk. She wouldn't subject herself to watching Dayton with another woman. The few minutes she had viewed were enough to add something of value to her research files.

Though she'd terminated the footage, she failed to do the same with her thoughts. Her mind wandered while she returned the disc and righted the floorboards.

If he had filmed Jasmine, had he filmed others?

She was certain he had not done that with her. Then again, she'd been asleep when he photographed her.

The metal on metal sound of a key twisting in the front door carried through the house as she staged the rug precisely in its previous position. She dove beneath the comforter, already constructing a cover story in her head. Her pulse evened out to its usual pace as she listened to the scoring of Dayton's arrival. The clomping of shoes and thunk of his keys being dropped on the coffee table.

Soon, he leaned against the doorjamb. "I thought you'd be up by now."

"I sleep in on the weekend. Occasionally."

He kicked off his hiking boots and sidled up to her, holding her as if everything about them was perfectly normal; but after the film screening, his embrace felt like a coffin surrounding her on all sides.

In his arms, she would die.

29

POLAROID GIRLS

Dayton

hough Lacey's investigation had quieted down, his relationship with Kenna had not seen much improvement.

Dayton thought about this while sitting at his desk at the rear of the practice. There was a positive correlation between the distance she'd put between them and his desperation to mend that rift. A pain splintered in his chest upon realizing it wasn't the universe or God or any other cosmic force tearing them apart. No, it was retribution for all he had done. Plain and simple.

Mary Janes clacked on the floor behind him and he shuffled papers, feigning productivity to cover the tracks of his brooding.

Kenna bent beside him to gather her things and he was assaulted with her scent. No matter how familiar that fragrant potion had become, he still tipped toward insanity every time he breathed her in. He'd had her so many times, flesh on flesh, and yet when their ephemeral contact reached its end, he was left hollow.

She spared very little of herself beyond the sheets and Dayton feared they were approaching end times.

"I'm heading out."

"It's 4 o'clock."

She slid a hand across her face. "I have a gynecology appointment, if you must know."

"Do you want me to take you?"

"No." Her brows pinched together. "I'll see you later, though, okay?"

He shook his head. "Tonight's not good for me. I'm behind on some paperwork."

She nodded, saying they would figure it out, and swept out of his office. Dayton may have been upset over her lack of parting affection but he was hyperaware of the state of their relationship.

He didn't have paperwork to catch up on nor did she have an appointment. Kenna had seen her OBGYN back in November. It had been notated on a digital calendar on her laptop, something he'd seen the night he let himself into her apartment. When she'd fled south to California to chat up his ex-fiancée. She was keeping something from him yet again.

What it was, he had no idea.

He toyed with the idea of following her but it wasn't a viable option. Another patient was due any minute.

Kenna

Liam had agreed to meet her downtown at Bigleaf. She ordered a latte she had no intention of drinking and gravitated toward the pair of armchairs in the corner of the shop. Kenna set her mug on the round coffee table and sat perfectly still, focusing on her breathing in an attempt to steady herself before Liam's arrival.

A few minutes later, he walked through the door and she was in awe of how much a year had changed him.

The shaggy hair was gone. Now it was short, spiked at the

front. He had traded his leather jacket and tight jeans for an oxford and slacks.

Liam gave her a half-wave and pointed to the register, a silent indication that he'd join her once he ordered his coffee.

Minutes later, he set his latte on the table and filled the chair adjacent to hers. They sat in a spell of silence that seemed to span days. Liam was the one to break it.

"I was a little more than surprised when you reached out. Didn't think I'd ever hear from you again." He gestured at her. "Let alone see you."

In that message, Kenna had not supplied a reason for their meeting but he hadn't needed one to accept. She wondered if that meant, on his end, their exchange in the cafe would serve as a kind of closure.

He shifted in the armchair, speaking again though she hadn't said a word. "I'm not sure how long I can stay. My job keeps me at the mercy of a phone call."

"Where do you work?"

"School district. IT. I float around wherever they need me. So much for my film degree, eh?" His cell phone chimed and he glanced at the screen. "I told my girlfriend I was here. She might pop over on her break. She works at the record store across the street." He slid the phone back in his pocket. "We met at a *Silence of the Lambs* screening. How's that for romantic?"

"Will told me she's picking up some of the slack for the trivia team."

"Well, Will told me that you brought a certain doctor to a party full of grad students. You're still hanging around that guy? I thought some of the novelty would've worn away by now."

"Liam—"

"Sorry. Really, it's none of my business who you're sleeping with." Hunching forward, he put his elbows on his knees. "Why did you want to see me? I mean, after all this time." He shrugged. "Why now?"

Kenna was thankful he'd posed the question, ten shades of relief flowing through her. She may not have had the courage to pluck the DVD from her bag otherwise.

She extended the disc to him over the coffee table and, though his eyes narrowed with suspicion, he accepted it.

"Where did you get this?"

"I can't tell you." But in saying that, Kenna had told him everything.

"*He* took this? Holy shit." Liam slumped in his chair, asking more quietly, "Was he the son of a bitch who slashed my tires?"

She nodded though it felt mechanical.

"I'm pretty sure."

"Why would he do that? That's insane."

"He wanted me. You were ..." she licked her lips, "in his way."

Was it so simple? It felt easier to believe it.

The bell tinkled above the shop's door and in walked a woman wearing platform sneakers. Several streaks of magenta highlighted her inky mop of hair. The sweater she wore had a wide neck and it revealed a further flash of skin as she bent to kiss Liam's cheek.

A moth was tattooed just below her collarbone.

Kenna had studied the Polaroids so many times, the names and faces were ingrained in her memory and that tattoo was unmistakable. She said the name without thinking.

"Ivy."

The woman straightened as her lips contorted into an uncertain smile. "That's me."

Liam opened his mouth to introduce them but she beat him to it.

"I'm Kenna. I'm a friend of Dayton's."

Ivy's smile vanished. "Don't say that fucker's name. And I don't know who you are, but you better not ever speak to me again."

. . .

Kenna pulled into her parking spot at her apartment complex, the wheel of her mind still spinning after the terse interaction with Liam and Ivy.

Just two days before, she'd found the explicit footage of Jasmine and then Ivy happened to be Liam's new love interest. She jerked the keys out of the ignition and closed her eyes, siphoning a breath.

It was as if the Polaroid girls were trying to find her, gravitating to her like she was an electromagnetic field. The current host for all their suffering. Yet she couldn't help but feel she'd brought on these lively hauntings.

She had been suspicious of Dr. Merino.

She had opened the box.

She had invited the women into her life.

Getting out of the station wagon, she started to step onto the walkway but her foot hovered above the pavement. Frozen midstep. Liza clunked down the steps, a large box bundled in her arms.

"Do you need help with that?"

Her roommate shifted the box and glanced at her, moving past her while muttering, "Shit."

Kenna's heart sank as she trailed Liza to her car and peered into the open trunk. It was filled with several of the same boxes and the sight sent her thoughts spinning like a weather vane. "Are you going somewhere?"

Her large, kind eyes brimmed with apology.

"I'm leaving."

Kenna laughed but Liza's expression remained. Waiting for the reality to sink in. "You can't be serious."

"I can't do this anymore, with your creepy boyfriend coming and going. Not after everything you've told me. Sometimes when he stops by, you aren't even home. I don't feel safe here."

Her throat closed up. Dayton had been coming by when she

wasn't there? The trunk slammed shut, making her jump slightly. She followed Liza to the driver's side door.

"I can't afford this place on my own."

Not only that, but she knew people wouldn't be lining up to take Liza's place. She'd slept with the school shrink and had become the joke of the university. Of the town.

Hand furled around the door handle, Liza whispered, "I'm really sorry, Ace."

Kenna stood in the parking lot, going numb from head to toe as she watched her back out of the space and drive away from the complex.

March

30

PRAYERS

*D*ays of begging and pleading had produced a most miraculous result. Dayton's presence beside her in one of St. James' pews at Wednesday evening Mass.

Though he was a reluctant parishioner, he blended in among the rest. He had grown up in the church and he understood the rituals, knew the routines. Kenna's chest fluttered each time he bowed his head, the epitome of stoicism as he mumbled along with the prayers. His hand laced through hers as they sang Gloria and the setting sun illuminated the stained-glass windows, bathing the nave in warm light.

The scene was ordinary, everyday, yet Kenna found it hopelessly romantic. For the first time in months, she felt safe and secure. Her mind was at ease with Dayton at her side as the priest delivered his sermon.

"Thanks for coming, really. It means a lot," Kenna said as they rose and exited their pew.

His hand found her lower back, gently guiding her along. His breath tangled in her hair. "Anything for you."

They emerged in the aisle and she turned to face Dayton, producing a tired smile all the while wishing she had more to give.

Professor Scott and a woman she presumed to be his wife approached them. Her dress was taut over her slightly rounded stomach.

"Man, I must be hallucinating." A wide grin brightened Professor Scott's face. "I'd love to hear how you managed to get him through these doors because I've been trying for years."

"I *was* raised Catholic."

"Exactly. Raised. That doesn't mean you stay that way."

"Hello to you too, Nate." Dayton adopted a sardonic tone. She always expected it to be accompanied by an eye roll but it never came. "Charlaine, this is Kenna."

While she hadn't minded being introduced that way to Carmen months earlier, the plainness of this introduction displeased her. Not 'my Kenna' or 'my girlfriend,' just Kenna.

Did she want the distinction of a title?

Something that defined their relationship, that web of sex and lies and indecipherable feelings neither of them could adequately decode.

"I've heard a lot about you," Charlaine said.

"Oh."

It was all she could think to say yet it made her sound like an idiot. She knew the Scotts were close friends of Dayton's and she resented the fact that she'd already embarrassed herself in their company.

"We're heading to dinner. Would you like to join us?"

"That would be wonderful."

Wonderful? Now she sounded too formal. Dayton smirked at her stuffy language and mumbled something in agreement.

They drove separately and met inside the restaurant, a cozy yet upscale place on the edge of town. Kenna had never been there and if it weren't for her church clothes she would've felt out of place in the enforced dress-code environment.

Though she didn't know Charlaine, there was an air of familiarity about her. A quality she had seen in her own mother's face time and time again that revealed far more than the snug fit of her clothing.

She felt sure enough to ask.

"How far along are you?"

"28 weeks." Her expression contorted into one of surprise. "I didn't think my bump was that noticeable."

Kenna shook her head. "It's in your face. My mom always looked the same way."

"Big family?"

"Huge. All girls."

Something pulled in her gut as she spoke of her family. She knew she needed to call them—it had been far too long.

But she couldn't bring herself to do it.

They had not spoken in years and she had ignored their excessive calls leading up to Thanksgiving. What would they say if she called them out of the blue? She knew what they'd say, no matter how much time had passed or how fervently she'd ignored them.

Come home.

That was her sisters' collective plea and Kenna supposed she was deserving of some reprimand from God for denying their earnest request. Perhaps that was Dayton's purpose in her life: this unsavory thing that would be used in her final judgment. She imagined that the notion was true, her path to Heaven or Hell determined not by her faith but by her familial neglect and an ill-advised relationship.

"We could leave right now and they wouldn't notice," Professor Scott said.

She offered a phony smile but it fell quickly as she sipped her water and arrived at a puzzling realization. Dayton had obviously known that his friends were expecting a child, so why had he kept the news from her? Wasn't that what people did when they were close? Shared details of their lives and developments from friends and family?

Pain ruled Kenna's chest. She and Dayton did not fit the text-book definition of close. They'd been perfect strangers, thrown together out of obligation, and their romance had blossomed only from the seeds of his obsession and her determination.

A darker thought took hold.

Maybe he didn't love her, had never loved her, but strung her along as some sick way of keeping her quiet.

Dayton's phone chimed within his slacks and she watched him slide it out halfway, though the screen was beyond her vantage point. He replaced it in his pocket, rising with unnatural haste. "Sorry to be so impolite, but I have to run to the hospital. It's a bit of a rocky situation."

He seemed to emphasize the last part and a strange yet undeniably smug look came over Professor Scott.

"Go do whatever you have to do. We'll drop Kenna off when we're done here."

Some secret knowledge laced their tones and it made her uneasy. There was a truth behind their words, one which they did not want uncovered. She was assaulted by thoughts of her conversation with Audrey, the merciless cycle of infidelity, and she wondered if Dayton had gotten too comfortable with her and it was starting up again.

"So, how long have you two been together? I've asked the guys but they aren't much for that kind of stuff," Charlaine said.

Together.

It was too nice a descriptor for what they had.

"We've never really been official."

"Well, I've known Dayton for a long time and I've never seen him with a girlfriend. He seems happier, don't you think, Nate?"

"Oh, yeah."

Charlaine stood and Professor Scott moved to help her but she playfully swatted his hand away. "I'll be back in a few."

Kenna felt a little awkward being left alone at a table in the middle of a crowded restaurant with one of her former professors but there was no sense in objecting to the arrangement.

"What's up with this guy who's been following Dayton around?"

She knew precisely who he was referring to but she played dumb. The last thing Professor Scott needed was to find out one of his dearest friends was a suspect in a homicide investigation.

"What guy?" The lie fell so easily from her lips. It seemed she was lying to everyone, herself included.

"Are you doing okay? You seem tired or something. Hell, I remember how you were in class. Spry is your middle name."

Kenna laughed and it breathed new life into her. Gave feeling to all that was numb.

"Not so great, actually. My roommate left. I hardly got a goodbye and she was gone." Swallowing, she considered how much she wanted to reveal. "I can't afford the apartment on my own and thanks to my ... reputation, I haven't had any luck finding a new roommate. I don't know what to do."

"That's rough," Professor Scott conceded. "Why don't you see if you can get out of the lease early, crash at Dayton's for a while? I know he wouldn't mind having you around."

"He doesn't know."

"You're going to tell him, though, right? He can help you."

Kenna internalized his words. Was he overcompensating for something, perhaps whatever Dayton had run off to take care of?

"No." She let out a small sigh. A tired, defeated sound. "Please, don't tell him about any of this."

His cheeks inflated before he released the air, nodding.

Charlaine soon returned and the three of them made polite conversation throughout dinner. By the minute, Kenna grew more and more resentful of the empty chair at her side.

April

31
BLINK

Kenna

A wave of memories drowned Kenna as she entered The Rusted Monkey. The exposed pipes and fairy lights and the bar that nearly cut across the length of the space. She'd spent many Thursdays in the bar. Talking, laughing, drinking. The scenes were far away, foreign almost. Distorted by time.

Will ran up to her as soon as she was through the door, mumbling as they walked along the aisle, "You should know, I didn't tell anyone you were coming."

"Why not?" she shot back.

"I was worried no one would show."

Dayton eyed her curiously from his and Nathan's post at the end of the bar.

She hadn't told him she was coming, either.

They approached the wooden booth, where the other members of the Barenaked Philosophers each wore wildly differing expressions. Neutrality masked Rebecca's face, at first, but a delayed sort of joy spread and softened her features. Liam's forehead furrowed but the glimmer in his eyes insisted that he was conflicted by her presence. Ivy was the easiest to read and the first to speak.

But not to Kenna.

She turned to her boyfriend, hostile. "Did you know about this?"

Liam started lamely sputtering a response but Will swooped in and saved him.

"Your boy didn't have anything to do with this. I invited her. Though, I'll admit, Ivy, if I had known you'd react like *this*, I would've invited Kenna a lot sooner."

She and Will slid into Rebecca's side of the booth. Ivy scowled at her while Liam remained quiet, passive, color flooding his cheeks.

Eyes narrowed, Dayton's gaze flicked between herself and Will before slamming back the rest of his—water?

When had he stopped drinking? Perhaps the more troubling question was why. He'd had a cardiology appointment a while back but he hadn't breathed a word about the results of the visit.

Will folded his arms atop the table and she knew the smug look he wore forewarned disaster for whatever came out of his mouth. "Judging by how pissed off you are, I'm guessing you already know that Kenna and your b.f. were almost a thing, once upon a time."

Liam served him a stare that could've cut glass and insinuated that, no, she had not known. Kenna found herself wondering if he and Ivy had discussed the tense Bigleaf interaction at length. Surely, he would have wanted to know why his girlfriend had lost her cool over a casual mention of Dr. Merino. Liam must have thought himself unlucky, this doctor tainting all of the women he was interested in.

"And the world gets smaller and smaller," Ivy said.

"More like stranger and stranger."

That brief exchange hung in the air and, for the few seconds their eyes met, something haunting and all at once familiar passed between them.

Everyone else at the table regarded them as if they were in another dimension and the conversation quickly shifted to the outcome of the prior trivia night.

Once they had debated the answer to the first question and submitted their card, Ivy excused herself. Kenna watched, chest tense, as she wandered straight past Dayton and Nathan, along the hallway that housed the bathrooms and the entrance to the kitchen. She kept going until she reached the rear exit, shoving the door's metal bar and escaping into the night. Kenna slowly counted down from 10 in her head before she slipped out of the booth and followed her, not bothering to give her teammates an excuse. Whatever she said would've been a lie.

To her surprise, she found Ivy with a cigarette wedged between two trembling fingers, shakily bringing it to her lips and inhaling. Ivy looked straight at her and exhaled a large plume of smoke in her face. Kenna immediately coughed and waved her hand to dispel the fumes as well as the stench, but both lingered as Ivy continued smoking.

"Listen," she exhaled another cloud, eyes trained on the brick building. "I don't know what you want from me, but we're sure as fuck not about to be all *Sisterhood of the Traveling Pants* just because we happened to sleep with the same crazy doctor."

She contemplated telling Ivy about the other girls for precisely one second. It was obvious she had trouble keeping her emotions level and that alone ruled her out as someone who could be trusted with such damning information.

Kenna decided on a gentle approach.

"What did he do to cause this kind of reaction? All I did was mention his name and—"

"I trusted him and he betrayed that."

She waited for a beat. "How?"

"He drugged me."

All of the blood drained from her veins. Kenna had suspected, during the height of drunkenness and paranoia, that Dayton had drugged her the first time she'd gone to his house but she'd been quick to dismiss the disorientation and slew of other symptoms.

Ivy extinguished the cigarette with the toe of her boot. She crossed her arms and leaned against the brick. "I mean, I don't have any proof, but I know he did it, you know?"

Kenna knew exactly what she meant but she had no intention of telling her that.

"What the hell was that at the coffee shop, by the way?"

"What do you mean?" Again, she knew.

Playing dumb wouldn't help.

"Please. I saw the way you looked at my tattoo before you looked at my face, like you were solving some puzzle."

She took a deep breath but it did nothing to steady her. Ivy already bordered on being unhinged. She could only imagine what her reaction would be to what she said next.

"I found a picture of you. In his house."

"What kind of picture?"

When Kenna didn't answer, she filled in the blanks.

"Oh, you've got to be fucking kidding me. You are, right?"

"I'm really sorry," she said quietly, adding, "There's one of me too."

"Just us?"

So much for not telling her about the other girls.

"11, if you include us."

"God. I knew there was something fucked up about him but I could never figure out what it was." Ivy produced a humorless laugh. "I'll admit, this is way less menacing than anything I'd pictured."

Had she shared the same grim thoughts Kenna had in those early days? That he was capable of murder. Hauled limp bodies around in his station wagon. Dumped them in the forest. Those thoughts had come crawling back as soon as Detective Reynolds implied Dayton's possible involvement in Lacey's disappearance and subsequent death.

But she had been found in a dumpster, not in the woods. No prints had been found. That cleared him of suspicion, so why did her heart constantly ache when she considered that maybe he *was* involved?

Why had Reynolds trailed him for so long if there wasn't any new evidence?

"Get out while you can." Ivy pulled the door open but she hesitated. "I loved him and he didn't so much as blink when he cut me out of his life. He'll do the same to you."

32

LIKE YOU MEAN IT

Kenna

She filled out an appointment card for the last patient of the day and passed it along with a forced greeting, heaving a sigh of relief once they had gone.

Her job performance had been less than stellar that day. Ivy's smoke clouded her brain. With a disquieting clarity, Kenna relived their conversation over and over. Her tinny voice and hard looks. For all her hurt, she had not cried.

Ivy was past the point of tears.

She hadn't yet confronted him about the drugging. They were slaves to their routines and a deep exhaustion had compounded and left them with little energy—and fighting required so much.

Knocking to announce herself, she entered the psychotherapy room where Dayton remained despite his patient having left. His head was angled back against the top of the chair, both hands buried in his hair. He stirred slightly when she perched on one of his thighs and she wondered if he'd heard her come in.

A tic ruled his jaw, one which seemed to never go away, even when he spoke. "Are we alone?"

"Mercifully."

Her fingertips traced that tense line, trying and failing to relieve some of its tension. Kenna took one look at his weathered face and all she wanted to do was cure him of his fatigue.

Silently, she cursed that urge. She lived every day surrounded by reminders of his toxicity and yet she craved his poison all the more. The poison that had slithered into her bloodstream and made her resistant to his lies, his follies.

Bracing her hands on his chest, she leaned forward and claimed his lips. Their kiss was slow and tentative. It was tame though she found herself overwhelmed with desire, a burning hunger that insisted Dayton's lips were not enough. Her tongue slipped over his and she relished in its slickness, that familiar feeling. She surprised herself by threading her fingers in his thick hair, further deepening the kiss. Kenna felt heavy and lightheaded at the same time, ascending to some unidentified circle of euphoria. He pulled away, breathing already ragged.

"It's been a long time since you kissed me like that."

"Like what?"

A sadness played over his features that broke her. "Like you mean it."

Those words coupled with his face set her soul ablaze. Kenna undid the buttons on his shirt, methodically, as her mouth captured his once again. She fumbled with a few of them but she didn't let it discourage her.

Fully open, the fabric draped at his sides. She shifted in order to properly straddle Dayton's lap. Her hands found his lean stomach—the cold, bare skin—and he elicited a small gasp at the warmth of her palms. A branding iron in a snowbank.

She felt his icy flesh melting beneath her the longer her hands remained pressed to him and she was pleased that he was pleasured by such a simple touch.

His arms hooked around her and, as he stood, she rose with him. He brought Kenna to the velvet chaise and all but dropped her amid the plush cushions. Like an animal attacking its prey, Dayton yanked the button on her jeans and tore at the zipper. He was working them down her hips before her thoughts had time to catch up. Her heart fluttered in her chest, a caged butterfly, as he used his hands to part her legs. Even though a flimsy piece of fabric kept her from being on full display, she felt completely exposed beneath his gaze.

Sweat sealed her to the couch and, despite Dayton tugging off her underwear, all she could think of was whoever would sit in the imprint of her slicken backside the next morning.

He didn't tease her with his words or his touch.

Instead, he bowed his head like he had in the cathedral as his tongue sailed over her. She relaxed against the sensation, at being so profoundly intimate with the man she'd once labeled clinical and detached. Presently, they were almost as close as two people could get and something twisted low in her stomach as she remembered she loved him.

She loved him and he had no idea.

Meanwhile, Dayton displayed his love without fear. It shone in the fierceness of his eyes and the torturous slip of his tongue. And, how strange it was, having a lover who brought her simultaneous misery and happiness.

Kenna fell apart and by the time she'd collected herself he had joined her on the sofa. Legs splayed, he undid his belt and soon he was kicking his pants from around his ankles. She felt her throat bob when he removed his boxers. He wrapped a hand around himself, producing slow strokes. It was something she had witnessed a handful of times but the eroticism of the act hadn't waned.

"Come here. Come here where you belong."

His tone dripped with need and the command sent a jolt between her legs. She climbed onto him as if she were being timed, tearing her blouse over her head and tossing it on the floor. Heat rushed to her cheeks as she slowly took him in. Inch by inch. He groaned and Kenna ground her hips, encouraged by his response.

Everything questionable in her life faded into nothingness. There was only the fire blazing through her core.

With two fingers, he snapped her bra and tore it from her frame, freeing her breasts. But his eyes stayed glued to hers as she rode him, their heavy breathing thickening the air around them.

The moment it was over, their illusion of intimacy shattered. Kenna didn't linger for cuddling on the couch or offer cursory kisses. She crossed the room and, with her back to Dayton, started getting dressed. Her fingers fumbled with the button on her jeans, missing the notch every time.

"Did you drug me?" She focused on the blank white wall. It was the only way she could ask the question.

"What? When?"

His scoffed response changed her mood on a dime. Calm morphing into hostility.

"You know exactly when. The first time I went to your house. We had *dinner*. Did you or did you not drug me?"

"Did your pal Ivy turn you on to this?"

"Answer the question, Dayton."

This time last year, she would have been scared out of her wits to shout at him with such reckless abandon but she felt she'd gained some kind of footing as his lover and employee.

He looked her dead in the eye, unblinking, and she may have run into the street, half-clothed, if she weren't so desperate for answers.

"I put a couple drops of GHB in your wine."

"I watched you make our drinks."

"It was in the bottom of your glass before I poured the wine."

Arms wrapped around herself, Kenna sank to the floor in her bra and jeans. "Why would you do that? Why?"

"You were always so tense. I wanted us to have a relaxing evening together."

"Which apparently included raping me."

"I'll admit, I was hoping the drug made you more receptive to intimacy but I never planned to—"

"The way you say things sometimes." Kenna produced a hollow laugh like Ivy had in the alleyway. "You didn't plan to. What does that mean? You might have done it on a whim?"

"I never wanted to hurt you."

"No? Why wasn't that thought running through your head when you slammed me against a door and held me in a chokehold while I had *GHB* swimming through my system?"

The long-winded retort had her going blue in the face. She took a series of deep breaths but it didn't lessen the strain in her cheeks, her neck, and Lacey's face flashed through her head as Kenna came dangerously close to feeling like she was taking her final breath.

"I panicked. You were getting too close. I didn't want you to see … who I really am."

"Well, congratulations, because I have no clue. You drugged me. You drugged Ivy. Maybe you did kill Lacey. You're clearly capable of acting without feeling anything."

Tears clouded her vision the entire drive to her apartment but she didn't give them permission to fall. Kenna had shed far too many tears for Dayton—perhaps more for his lovers—and she would shed no more.

Pulling into the parking space, she regarded her reflection in the rearview mirror with an air of resoluteness.

She was going to be tougher. Grow a thicker skin.

Never mind the fact that an emotional slipup would cost them everything with the ongoing investigation.

Them. Kenna almost laughed but her throat already stung from suppressing tears and she thought it was unwise. Why did she care what happened to him? She should've been more concerned with protecting herself.

The suppression swelled within until, all at once, the emotion unleashed itself in a violent burst. She banged the heel of her palm against the steering wheel and pain soon blazed through her forearm.

"Damn my love for him." Softer, she cursed, "damn it all to Hell."

Following a moment of quiet composure, she summoned enough energy to get out of the station wagon. As she climbed the wooden stairs, she thought only of what would ease her mind and body after the day's troubling developments. A hot shower, the blissful cocoon of her down comforter. Solitude, above all.

But as Kenna neared the front door, self-care was rendered the least of her concerns.

Fingers trembling, she snatched the neon orange notice posted below the peephole. It felt like a sick practical joke. She read the paper but the details didn't make it any more real. Still, she must have registered its significance because the tears that she'd so valiantly restrained rushed forth as she sank to the welcome mat, crumpling the paper in a clenched fist.

Her eviction notice.

33

TAKE MY HAND

Dayton

*H*e sat in the back corner booth at Sinclair's, the same one he and Kenna had occupied the night their relationship truly began. He'd been breathing a little easier since Detective Reynolds crawled back to Portland with an unsolved investigation hanging over his head.

Not tonight.

His breathing was far from normal and his nerves were off the charts as he sweated against the vinyl, waiting for Kenna to show up. The ring box strained in his pocket and, for that reason, Dayton had already decided against standing to greet her and prayed she didn't take offense to the abnormal behavior.

Some of his anxiety quelled as she approached. Her hair hung wet and limp around her face. She hadn't dressed up for the occasion, clad in her usual jeans and blouse. He reminded himself that she wasn't aware of any occasion.

For her, it was an ordinary day.

Kenna didn't seem to mind his lack of greeting, offering a terse smile as she took her seat. Her waterlines were pink and swollen. She grabbed the wine list, oblivious that he had already ordered the same bottle they'd shared during their previous visit.

"Is everything alright?"

"Rough night." Her eyes cut to him. "I'd rather not talk about it."

The waiter brought the wine and uncorked it tableside. Dayton resented the fact that she carefully spied the inside of her glass before she let him fill it.

She studied him while taking a prolonged sip, seeming to note his meticulous appearance. He wore the dress shoes he had bought for Nathan's wedding the year before. He'd even gelled his hair, something he had not done since his residency graduation.

"You're wearing a tie?" Her voice climbed higher on the last syllable as amusement danced across her face.

"I'll confess, I didn't ask you here solely for dinner."

The playfulness vanished. Confusion wove her mouth into a frown and drew her eyebrows together.

"My darling." He seized her hand across the table, intertwining their fingers, and she looked at it as if it were severed and bleeding all over the tablecloth. "You are the single most important thing in my life, and loving you has given me a light that's always been absent."

Quiet fell over the room as other diners took interest in their romantic scene. Dayton rose, removed the ring box from his pocket and kneeled on the floor in front of her.

He opened it and Kenna turned white as a ghost.

There were no tears building in her eyes, no hand flying to her mouth in surprise. He went on anyway.

"Kenna Aisling O'Callaghan, will you marry me?"

Kenna

His question stabbed at her heart.

Stomach knotting, she regarded the ring seated pristinely

within its cushion. A square diamond lay at the center and smaller ones studded the braided band. It was far too gorgeous to represent something as ugly as their romance.

A hopeful spark electrified Dayton's eyes but she kept hers glued to the ring, that inanimate object that wouldn't try to gauge her expression or prod for an answer.

The man she loved was at her feet, asking for her hand, and all she felt was dread. Despite that love, she had agreed it'd be irresponsible to tie herself to him in any meaningful way.

And then it hit her.

They had never discussed having formally entered a relationship and yet he was proposing.

She remembered what Reynolds had said during her questioning, that Dayton had referred to her as his girlfriend. And, even though they were never official, it didn't strike her as odd until this moment. Audrey's words rang through her head. *This is moving too fast.*

"Sit down," she commanded in a whisper.

Everyone who had been on standby for applause went back to minding their own business as he returned to the booth, setting the closed box on the table.

Displeasure washed over him but he stayed quiet and waited for Kenna to speak. He drained his glass and refilled it, dark gaze fixed on her.

"Marriage, honestly?"

"Why can't you wrap your pretty head around the fact that I love you?"

"You may love me, but I know you." Her throat constricted as she lowered her voice. "How do you suppose I could so much as entertain accepting a proposal from you given that you may be a *murderer?*"

"Don't act so innocent. I know what you've been up to. You and your Nancy Drew crusades. Your trip to California. Your fake gynecology appointment. You've been rifling through my things, stealing DVDs. Tsk, tsk." Something sinister possessed him and she had flashbacks of the night he'd held her against his bedroom door, fearful that, if she went home with him after this disastrous dinner, things would be much worse.

Through it all, he kept his voice level. "If you want to keep things from me, I suggest you get better at hiding them."

Tense minutes passed without a word. All Kenna heard was the thudding of her heart in her empty chest.

"There's a part of you that thinks I did this. I also know there's a more prevalent part that loves me."

She'd never said the words and, somehow, he knew. But Dayton couldn't have actually known what it was like being in love with him. She felt like a balloon stretched to the limit with oxygen, trapping all of that airy lightness but having no room to breathe. Fearing sharp objects at every turn, something that had the power to deflate her modicum of happiness.

"What is this actually about?" she asked.

He was silent, searching her face in earnest, as if he were waiting for her to arrive at a conclusion. He didn't wait long.

Lips parting, he delivered a statement that chilled her to the bone. "Spouses can't testify against each other."

Her gut birthed an intense pain. A hand sprouted within, tearing and twisting at her insides. Bile rose and its acidity blazed a trail up her esophagus but she slammed her eyes shut and willed it to dispel.

Kenna looked at the sparkling ring. The tiny flecks of light casting off the diamonds blurred as her tears welled. She'd received the eviction notice from her landlord and now the prince of darkness was proposing. No matter that she loved him.

Marriage was unthinkable.

She didn't know if he was guilty and scared or innocent and simply manipulating her into accepting the offer, but as she drank in his face she arrived at her answer.

Though it defied all logic, she wanted only to help him.

Her voice quaked. "If we do this … if there's a trial, I want out afterward."

"I knew you would come to your senses." A faint smile tugged at the lines in his cheeks as he plucked the jewelry from its box, beckoning for her to extend her arm. "I've been dying to see how this would look on you."

Dayton seized her trembling hand with both of his and delicately slid the ring on her finger. It was beautiful, but as it lay against her skin, her head was filled with visions of a curse surging through her veins, blood turning black and coagulated. His intense stare was a bad trip from which she was reeling to escape but she was granted no relief as he placed a featherlight kiss on the inside of her wrist.

"You're mine now, lamb."

If you enjoyed the second installment of Confessional, please consider leaving it a review on Amazon, Goodreads, or your vendor of choice. Reviews help indie authors gain visibility and expand their readership.

Sign up for my newsletter to stay up to date on new releases, cover reveals, beta opportunities, and more!

ABOUT THE AUTHOR

Leighann Hart is the author of the Rosenfeld duet and the Confessional trilogy. She is a huge mental health advocate and this sometimes—okay, oftentimes—bleeds into her love stories.

She consumes heinous amounts of espresso and pays tithe daily to the New York Times Spelling Bee. Her biggest regret is that she probably will not meet Rick Moranis before he dies.

Leighann lives with her husband, daughter, and Sugar the Shetland Sheepdog in a convection oven—er, Georgia.

Connect with Leighann Online

www.leighannhart.com
leighanniswriting@gmail.com
Goodreads @ Leighann Hart
BookBub @ leighannhart

www.ingramcontent.com/pod-product-compliance
Lightning Source LLC
Chambersburg PA
CBHW030926210726
48290CB00007B/2084